Deedra felt a  **she was being**

Stalked. Targeted.

The glint flashed fr...... again. Suddenly a loud crash resounded from outside and the picture window exploded inward. She buried her scream in Beau's wide chest as glass rained into the room. Beau caught her in a bear hug and set her behind him out of harm's way.

He moved with stealth and grace. Another bullet crashed into the room. Wood paneling cracked. Deedra shrieked and scrambled into the kitchen. From her position she watched Beau activate the secret paneling beside the fireplace and pull his favorite hunting rifle from the depths of the storage wall lined with guns. She knew every gun was kept cleaned and loaded. Natural predators—grizzlies, cougars, rattlers and even coyotes—often wandered too near for safety. Deedra shivered.

This time the predator was human....

Dear Harlequin Intrigue Reader,

As you make travel plans for the summer, don't forget to pack along this month's exciting new Harlequin Intrigue books!

The notion of being able to rewrite history has always been fascinating, so be sure to check out *Secret Passage* by Amanda Stevens. In this wildly innovative third installment in QUANTUM MEN, supersoldier Zac Riley must complete a vital mission, but his long-lost love is on a crucial mission of her own! Opposites combust in *Wanted Woman* by B.J. Daniels, which pits a beautiful daredevil on the run against a fiercely protective deputy sheriff—the next book in CASCADES CONCEALED.

Julie Miller revisits THE TAYLOR CLAN when one of Kansas City's finest infiltrates a crime boss's compound and finds himself under the dangerous spell of an aristocratic beauty. Will he be the *Last Man Standing*? And in *Legally Binding* by Ann Voss Peterson—the second sizzling story in our female-driven in-line continuity SHOTGUN SALLYS—a reformed bad boy rancher needs the help of the best female legal eagle in Texas to clear him of murder!

Who can resist those COWBOY COPS? In our latest offering in our Western-themed promotion, Adrianne Lee tantalizes with *Denim Detective*. This gripping family-in-jeopardy tale has a small-town sheriff riding to the rescue, but he's about to learn one doozy of a secret.... And finally this month you are cordially invited to partake in *Her Royal Bodyguard* by Joyce Sullivan, an enchanting mystery about a commoner who discovers she's a betrothed princess and teams up with an enigmatic bodyguard who vows to protect her from evildoers.

Enjoy our fabulous lineup this month!

Sincerely,

Denise O'Sullivan
Senior Editor, Harlequin Intrigue

DENIM DETECTIVE
ADRIANNE LEE

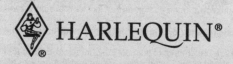

TORONTO • NEW YORK • LONDON
AMSTERDAM • PARIS • SYDNEY • HAMBURG
STOCKHOLM • ATHENS • TOKYO • MILAN • MADRID
PRAGUE • WARSAW • BUDAPEST • AUCKLAND

ISBN 0-373-22781-7

DENIM DETECTIVE

Copyright © 2004 by Adrianne Lee Undsderfer

This edition published by arrangement with Harlequin Books S.A.

® and TM are trademarks of the publisher. Trademarks indicated with ® are registered in the United States Patent and Trademark Office, the Canadian Trade Marks Office and in other countries.

www.eHarlequin.com

Printed in U.S.A.

ABOUT THE AUTHOR

When asked why she wanted to write romance fiction, Adrianne Lee replied, "I wanted to be Doris Day when I grew up. You know—singing my way through one wonderful romance after another. And I did. I fell in love with and married my high school sweetheart and became the mother of three beautiful daughters. Family and love are very important to me, and I hope you enjoy the way I weave them through my stories." Adrianne also states, "I love hearing from my readers and am happy to write back. You can reach me at Adrianne Lee, P.O. Box 3835, Sequim, WA 98382. Please enclose a SASE if you'd like a response."

Books by Adrianne Lee

HARLEQUIN INTRIGUE
296—SOMETHING BORROWED, SOMETHING BLUE
354—MIDNIGHT COWBOY
383—EDEN'S BABY
422—ALIAS: DADDY
438—LITTLE GIRL LOST
479—THE RUNAWAY BRIDE
496—THE BEST-KEPT SECRET
524—THE BRIDE'S SECRET
580—LITTLE BOY LOST
609—UNDERCOVER BABY
627—HIS ONLY DESIRE
678—PRINCE UNDER COVER
696—SENTENCED TO WED
781—DENIM DETECTIVE

Don't miss any of our special offers. Write to us at the following address for information on our newest releases.

Harlequin Reader Service
U.S.: 3010 Walden Ave., P.O. Box 1325, Buffalo, NY 14269
Canadian: P.O. Box 609, Fort Erie, Ont. L2A 5X3

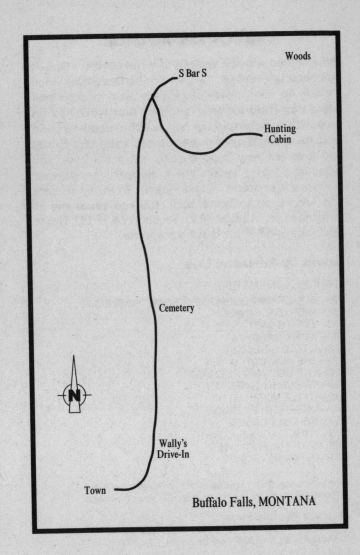

Woods

S Bar S

Hunting
Cabin

Cemetery

Wally's
Drive-In

Town

Buffalo Falls, MONTANA

CAST OF CHARACTERS

Beau Shanahan—A snap decision has brought a killer bent on revenge into this small-town sheriff's life. Someone who wants an eye for an eye. Someone who causes Beau's daughter's death, then comes gunning for his wife.

Deedra Shanahan—Fear of a killer drives Beau's wife to take extreme actions.

Callie Shanahan—Has this two-year-old really been snatched?

Floyd Mann—This former white supremacist exacts revenge for his wife's accidental death.

Nora Lee Anderson—Is she the rookie cop she purports to be, or is that just her cover?

Heck Long—Beau's deputy takes things at face value, which makes him more hindrance than help.

T. R. Rudway—A legal eagle too upscale for the likes of Buffalo Falls.

Luanne Pine—Beau's office worker is grieving the loss of her best friend, but she might be more lethal than ditzy.

Dr. Elle Warren—A psychologist who is as obsessive as some of her patients.

For my mother, Virginia Lee "Pete" Pozzi.
I was blessed to be your daughter.
I will never forget you. Or stop missing you.

Special thanks to Denise O'Sullivan,
whose support and understanding through a difficult
time in my life has made things easier for me at every
turn. Also, to Anne Martin, Gayle Webster
and Mary Alice Mierz—who all know why.

Prologue

"Cabin looks deserted," the deputy said.

"Yeah, well, looks can be deceiving." No one knew that better than Beau Shanahan. He glared at the backwoods Montana shack, hate a dark shadow on his heart. He'd lost everything that ever mattered to the cop-killing, family-wrecking scumbag who owned this pile of reject scrap.

It was payback time.

"Remember, we need him alive," he cautioned, taking the lead as he motioned for his men to move in. The rustle of bodies creeping through the underbrush might be the wind; the scurrying of feet over the rocky ground no noisier than a rattler slithering through a dry riverbed. They all had reasons for wanting this fugitive, but no one had more than Beau.

He stepped with the feral instinct of a stalking panther, with a wild sense of invulnerability, as though he could smell his prey on the air.

"Mann!" He reached the porch first. "Floyd Mann!"

The silence was broken by the cocking of seven rifles.

"Montana State Police! Coming in!" His boot heel

rammed the door frame. Wood cracked. His second kick sent the door splintering inward, and Beau slammed headlong through it as though he were invincible. As bulletproof as his Kevlar vest. "Don't try going out the back, Mann! You're surrounded!"

The inside of the cabin was filled with murky light and stank of cold wood fires and bacon fat. The furniture consisted of a pinochle-size table, two straight-back chairs, two rockers and a sideboard, all crudely handmade. Beau dashed to the second room, half expecting to hear Mann scrambling out the back window despite Beau's warning. But the other room was as empty as the main area. The whole place had the feel of a space long abandoned. As though Mann hadn't been here in a damned long time.

But he'd been seen.

Yesterday.

By a reliable eyewitness.

Heck Long, the only one of Beau's deputies too quick to judge on face value, clambered into the cabin and took his own quick tour. He sighed. "Another dead end."

"No." Beau wouldn't accept that. "He's here… somewhere. Has to be."

"If so, he's gone invisible." Heck's rifle slumped to the floor, looking as dejected as the deputy himself.

Another deputy came inside, followed by the others. Heck looked inside the stove. "Ashes are colder than a witch's teat. If Mann's been stayin' here, he's got the blood of a snake."

There was a strange look in Heck's eyes, in the eyes of all six of the men, as though they wished Beau would give it up. He knew they thought he was taking too many risks, leading them on one wild-goose chase after another. They thought he was *obsessed* with running Floyd Mann to ground, as though Beau were one of the "crazies" this job attracted.

Like that letter-writing nutcase whose delusion revolved around a love affair between herself and Beau that existed only in her mind. Like "the confessor" who claimed responsibility for every major crime that came along from mugging to murder. Like the ufologist who claimed to see strange lights in the woods around the S bar S ranch.

Like Mann, a former white supremacist bent on vengeance.

Fury spiked through Beau, hot and hard as steel. He embraced it. Let it lace his words. "Go check the outbuildings. The lot of you. But just in case Mann's the snake you claim—watch your step. We all know about his fangs, but chances are he has booby traps. Hidey-holes."

The moment he was alone, Beau blew out a heavy breath. "Obsessed, my ass."

Yes, obsessed. Deedra's taunt resounded in his head, an echo from the past, an accusation cast in the heat of desperation and despair. Two of the last words his wife had ever said to him. As sorry as he was about that, it didn't mean she'd been right.

No, he wasn't hunting Mann any harder than he would any other perp who ran around killing state troopers in a personal war of revenge and who'd caused Beau to lose his only two reasons for living.

Heeding his own caution of hidey-holes and booby traps, he held his rifle at the ready and scanned every inch of the cabin's main room. The wood-burning stove provided both the means of heat and cooking. A tarnished silver coffeepot hugged one edge and an iron skillet hung above on a nail pounded into the wall.

The room was bare of personal items. No signs of recent use. No newspapers. Or magazines. Clever of Mann not to leave anything that would allow them to pinpoint *when* he'd been here. But he was also careless, Beau realized, noting the clean spot on the dusty shelf used for canned goods.

Mann *had* been here.

Recently.

Beau moved into the bedroom, his boot heels hitting the hardwood flooring with a hollow thud, despite his wary steps. There was a double bed against one wall, the linen stripped and put away, likely in one of the dresser drawers. A closet was set in the opposite wall. Near the foot of the bed stood a hand-carved cradle. Beau froze at the sight of it. From where he stood, he could see a blanket poking from the high edges and swore he saw tiny fingers gripping the silk trim. *Callie*. His breath woofed from him as if he'd been gut punched, and a painful, awful hope leaped from the darkest recesses of his being.

Had Mann stolen his little girl four months ago? Was she here…in this cradle?

He rushed to the baby bed. Touched the teeny splayed fingers. Felt cold rubber. He flinched. Repulsed. A doll. The size of an eighteen-month-old toddler. Callie's size. A cry died in his throat. He cursed, kicking the cradle to clatter away from him. Then he shook himself. A booby trap. Meant to stop him in his tracks. To make him vulnerable. To show him he could be caught off guard.

His face clenched as he swung toward the closet, bringing the rifle up with him. He toed open the door, trigger finger taut. He stared into the dark niche, a space as small as the coat closet in the foyer of the Shanahan ranch house. No place for a white supremacist the size of Mann to hide. A worn trench coat in camouflage print draped a wire hanger, its hem brushing a pair of military boots. Beau's gaze stilled. *Muddy* boots. He hunkered to his haunches for a better look. Not boots with dried caked mud, but damp mud.

If Mann had gone, it hadn't been long ago.

He scanned the closet once more, spying an attic access above the storage shelf. Was Mann overhead? Peering down on him? He fetched one of the straight-backed chairs and stood on the seat. With the nose of the gun, he pushed the trap door aside, waited a breath or two, gathered his courage and the gun and hoisted himself up and over the edge. He strained to adjust to the dimmer light and to hear any noise within or from below, aware that this too could be a booby trap.

Grabbing the flashlight at his waist, he swung the bright beam over cobwebs, bat guano and enough dust to convince him nothing human had been up here in ages.

He dropped to the floor with a panther's stealth. He was missing something. He knew it as surely as he knew his own name. But what?

He studied the bedroom again. Not seeing *it*. But as he started toward the doorway into the main room, it occurred to him that the bed was at an odd angle. Why? *My boot heels hit the hardwood flooring with hollow thuds.* Hollow. His gaze fell to the floor, and he sank to his knees. *Aha.* A secret hatch, almost invisible, given the spacing and makeup of the floorboards, had been cut between the planks. He moved the bed, the metal frame scraping across the floor.

"You down there, Mann? Cornered like the rat you are?"

He levered the hatch up and kicked it to the wall. A ladder led down into a pitch-black earthen pit. As Beau pulled his flashlight from his waistband, a sudden movement in the darkness startled him. He dropped the flashlight, but before he could get the rifle to his shoulder, Floyd Mann fired. The bullet burned through Beau's unprotected flesh. He went down hard, the back of his head slamming the floor.

As his world stretched away from him his inner vision filled with images of his wife and child, both gone at Mann's hand. In that last moment of consciousness he understood he *had* been obsessed with finding Mann. Understood why he'd *needed* to find him.

Killing Mann wouldn't bring back Callie and Deedra, but Mann killing him had freed Beau of his endless misery.

And Beau smiled.

Chapter One

Beau's leg ached like a son of a bitch. Mann. Still out there. Still after the troopers involved in that high-speed pursuit. Still intent on avenging the deaths of his wife and unborn child.

Freakin' bastard hadn't ended Beau's life, though, just his run with the State Troopers. The bullet had torn through his calf, wiped out muscle and tissue—as well as leaving him with a limp that would likely be life-long—but had missed every major artery. Damn Mann. *He knew I'd be wearing body armor. That was a given. So why didn't he aim for my head? Or anywhere else that would've ended this eternal misery?*

"These new Wanted posters just arrived. Thought you might like a glance at them." Luanne Pine entered his office carrying a sheaf of papers. She had an oval face with pale skin against a mass of coffee-brown hair. Her guileless aqua gaze was probative behind wire-rimmed glasses. The frown made her appear younger than her twenty-five years. "Something the matter, Sheriff?"

Beau blinked at the title that still fit him like a new

Stetson, stiff, yet to be broken in. Floyd Mann might have closed a door for him, but a window had opened right behind it. Buffalo Falls, Montana, had been the hometown of every Shanahan in Beau's family for the past one hundred years. And every one of those years had seen a DeMarco in the sheriff's position. But Clyde DeMarco had been the last of his line, and with his passing six weeks ago, the good townsfolk had elected Beau to take his place.

With the job, he'd inherited Luanne. Dispatcher. File clerk. Secretary. Receptionist. She hadn't been here much longer than Beau, but knew more about running his new office than he did. Not that there was much to know. The whole of the Buffalo Falls police force consisted of: Beau; Nora Lee Anderson, rookie patrol person, whose résumé also included sharp shooter, sketch artist and fingerprinter; Heck Long, who'd followed Beau from the state level to small-town obscurity like a misguided lap dog; and Luanne.

He glanced at the pages she'd spread before him, rubbing his sore leg, wishing he could reach inside himself and assuage the ache in his heart. "Why would you think something's the matter?"

Luanne shrugged her slim shoulders. "You look as unhappy as a child who's just had his birthday party called off."

Beau felt the blood drain from his face. If she'd stabbed him in the chest, she couldn't have done a better job of tearing at his already grated heart. Today would have been his daughter's second birthday.

"It's nothing." His throat tightened against the hurtful lie. "Just my leg."

"Oh, my, well, isn't it about time to take your pain pills?"

He glanced at the clock. "You're right. Thanks."

"Hey, no problem." She filled a paper cup with water from the bottle by the door and brought it to him. "It's also time for my appointment…unless you need something else?"

Beau accepted the water and took his pills. "Naw, you run along."

"Good. Dr. Warren doesn't like to be kept waiting," Luanne said, and Beau nodded, understanding.

Dr. Warren had been his wife's grief counselor, too. Luanne had lost her best friend last year. Deedra, her child. *His child.* Maybe Luanne felt better spilling her guts about her heartache, but it hadn't helped Deedra. If anything, Dr. Warren had pushed her farther into the land of delusion and deepened Beau's disdain for the whole head-shrinking profession.

Besides, he couldn't verbalize his grief. Not even to Deedra. He'd handled the death of their daughter *his* way, kept his own counsel…and driven his wife away. God, but the world seemed overloaded with sorrow these days.

"I've got some errands to run, too. Heck can handle things while we're gone." He levered his cane and rose from behind his desk. At the door he snatched his Stetson from the coatrack. "In fact, after your appointment, why don't you go home and spend the rest of the day with your little boy."

"Little girl."

"Pardon?"

"I have a little girl." Luanne was a single parent, forced to move back in with her mother after her divorce. She beamed at him. "Jess."

Beau grimaced. "My sexist attitude is showing. I assumed Jess was a boy's name."

"That's okay. You aren't the first."

Beau bade her goodbye and headed outside to talk to Heck, but couldn't help wondering if Luanne realized how lucky she was to have a little girl. Stupid thought. One only had to look into her eyes as she spoke of the child to know that. Beau thought of Callie, of the way he'd always lighted up when speaking of her, and his heart bled. "God, Deedra, where are you?"

WISHING SHE HAD a heating pad and a fistful of Extra Strength Tylenol, Deedra Shanahan rubbed at her lower back. She wanted to reach inside herself and extract the pain, toss it away and restore the well-being of a body that had betrayed her, that had sent her mentally spiraling into some dark place where family and friends could not reach.

It amazed her that something as small as a noncancerous uterine fibroid tumor could cause such vast physical and mental distress. The doctors had said a hysterectomy could resolve the problem and drag her from the edge of insanity.

But could it?

She'd come close to finding out. Been on the surgery table. Prepped. Anesthetized.

An IV needle away from being infused with the wrong blood.

Deedra shuddered at how close she'd come to not surviving this latest attempt on her life. She cast a wary gaze over the cars behind and ahead of her rented Subaru, aware of a slight tremor in her hands. She'd felt safe, anonymous on Interstate 90, but turning off at Butte and heading southeast on SR2 brought back not only familiar scenery, but the sense of dread she'd awakened with that morning.

Had it been only two months since she'd gone? Since she'd thought running away would end the constant threat? The constant fear. She'd run as far as she could and begun to build a new life, a false life based on lies. But *he* had kept looking. Had found her. Had tried killing her…again.

Floyd Mann.

Although Beau hadn't believed it, *she knew*. Mann wanted Beau to suffer the way *he* was suffering. To that end, he'd taken the one thing that mattered most to her and Beau. That hadn't been enough for Mann. It hadn't been enough that he'd driven her and Beau further apart, that he'd pushed her to an act of desperation that probably had ramifications she couldn't even imagine.

Didn't want to imagine.

Mann wouldn't be happy until Beau's wife was as dead as his own.

There had been too much death. It had to stop. Deedra had to stop it. Not by running away, not by falling back on tactics of deception, of bait and switch, but by facing up to all that had occurred and dealing with it. By coming back to the small town of Buffalo Falls, coming home to the S bar S ranch. Facing Mann head-on. Facing her grief.

Facing Beau.

Making him believe. Making him help.

Another shudder swept her body, drawing an inconsolable ache through her heart and a slash of pain through her lower back. She needed to reschedule the surgery as soon as possible. But the medical procedure wouldn't cure the worst of what ailed her. She rubbed her back again. The largest part of her pain wasn't physical, wasn't hormonal upheaval, but unrelenting grief. For all that she'd lost—from her newfound belief that *she* actually deserved something good in life—to Beau, to Callie...

Callie's image sprang into her mind. Plump, rosy cheeks, cherry-bowed mouth, curly black hair and round green eyes so like Beau's. Her chubby fingers reaching out with trust, her laugh a musical chime. Deedra breathed in the cloying scent of fresh roses from the bouquet on the back seat and swallowed with difficulty, tears stinging her eyes at the thought of her little girl...the only baby she would ever have.

She would have been two years old today.

"Oh, Callie." She touched her lips, holding in the sob. Her daughter had been the one thing Deedra had never been—wanted by her parents. Callie had been conceived in love, a rich, lush love that Deedra had once believed nothing could destroy. But the love she'd counted on had been as fragile as their little girl, as vulnerable to outside influences and enemies as Deedra herself had once been.

She tried shaking off this dark musing, but it seemed an impossible task. Could anything really ease the pain of grief and loss? Counseling hadn't done a damned bit of good. Passing time? Hah! Sure, today the shock wasn't as raw as last month. As startling. But the ache in her heart never left. Like a fresh wound the pain throbbed so intensely she wanted to cry out from the hurt.

As she exited the main road and started down the slope to the river, a wide expanse of green water and white rapids curiously called "the creek" by everyone in Buffalo Falls, Deedra thought of her counselor's theory. The searing heartache was God's way of reminding Deedra of the precious gift she'd been granted in Callie, a way that ensured she'd never forget.

The suggestion still infuriated her. *As if I'd ever forget Callie.*

She slowed the car, accommodating the speed limit as she crossed the bridge into the town she'd called home since marrying Beau Shanahan three years ago. "Population twenty-five hundred give or take," a hand-painted sign proclaimed. The business section was laid out like a tic-tac-toe game with three main arteries running its twelve-block length and three more its width. Two-story, brick-fronted buildings with picture-size glass display windows made up Main Street, offering everything from insurance to ladies' dresses to auto parts and Granny Jo's Home Cooking.

Most of the vehicles angled against the stretch of sidewalks this Monday morning consisted of battered and dusty pickup trucks or SUVs—the work force of this ranching and farming community. None of the vehicles would be locked. Some would have keys dangling from ignitions. Before moving here, she'd never known the kind of trust Buffalo Falls citizenry took for granted.

The town had become her haven, her sanctuary...until Mann.

She hit the outskirts, drove past the new grocery store and Wally's Hamburger Shack, picking up speed as the road wound through rolling fields of golden hay and rocky pastures, dotted with scrub pines and Angus cattle.

For every good memory this town embodied, it also roused her saddest, most dire nightmares—the worst of which was the sense that Callie lived and needed only to be found. She'd prayed she'd put that crazy notion behind her. She had purposely driven the long way to the S bar S, through town, to avoid the accident site.

And yet, every familiar inch of road that stretched beneath her tires brought the awful hope, the terrible post-traumatic sensation that if she could relive that day she could change its outcome.

Turn back the clock. Relive the past. Yeah, right. That was crazy talk. Absolute madness.

The fact that she could even *think* such things squelched the teeny doubt she'd still harbored about facing Beau. She needed his help to accept Callie's death. To get on with her life.

To get Mann out of their lives.

Headstones loomed ahead, rising in an irregular pattern from the hillside. She slowed to a crawl and drove between two whitewashed brick pillars. A paved roadway spread like a network of veins through the cemetery, allowing access to several different areas of burial ground.

As she approached the final resting place of the Shanahan clan, she spied a man hunkered down before a pink marble marker. His wavy raven hair glistened in the sunlight. Her pulse gave a sudden leap of recognition, and her heart accelerated to a mixed beat of joy and fear. This wasn't what she'd envisioned, not how she'd imagined their initial encounter, but fate seemed to have other ideas.

Ready or not, the time had come.

She parked, gathered the bouquet from the back seat and began wending her way through the tombstones. She cautiously scanned the cemetery for Mann, forcing her resistant feet to move toward the lone figure, knowing he was standing before the grave she sought.

Callie's grave.
Her *empty* grave.

BEAU FEATHERED his fingers over the tombstone he'd had erected for his baby daughter, her life cut short in its eighteenth month. All of their futures altered irredeemably with her disappearance; all of their dreams and hopes as gone as she. He felt his heart in his throat, and his mind filled with the image of that damned Jeep on its side, of Deedra near dead behind the wheel, of Callie's baby seat empty.

Beau raised himself on his cane. His leg ached with renewed vengeance, as if he hadn't taken anything to alleviate the pain.

His heart ached worse.

He deserved to face this day alone. He should have shown Deedra compassion. Tried to understand her need to believe Callie was still alive…instead of insisting she accept that a toddler couldn't have survived in those woods at night. Damn it all. He should have anticipated her reaction to his emotional distancing, should have realized she'd take it as abandonment…given her history.

He should have known she was so depressed, so distraught, she'd take herself out of the misery. He had no idea where she'd gone. Had heard not one word from her since she'd left. For all he knew, she was dead too.

He choked on the thought.

"Beau?"

He froze, a shiver scraping his spine. God, he was losing it, missing Deedra so much he was actually hearing her speak his name. He wanted it to be her so much, he couldn't swallow. He clutched the handle of his cane harder, needing balance, both mentally and physically.

He blamed Mann for her leaving, but in truth, the blame was his. He'd been so obsessed with running that lowlife cop killer to the ground, so wrapped up in his grief at losing Callie, he hadn't had anything left for Deedra.

"Beau?"

This time he jerked around and almost went down on his bad leg. A woman stood not five feet from him, holding a bouquet of pink baby roses. He blinked trying to focus, but couldn't believe what he saw. He rubbed at his eyes and looked again. It was Deedra's face, her wide, heavily lashed gray eyes, her slightly freckled, upturned nose, her lush full lips, her dimpled chin. But there were also differences. No wild mane of wavy burnished-copper hair—only a snowy-blond cap with wisps feathering her temples and forehead. And she was thinner than Deedra, the hollows beneath her cheekbones pronounced.

It wasn't her.

"Beau, I—"

That distinct, throaty voice shredded through his denial like claws through sheer gauze. No woman he'd ever met shared Deedra's raspy, sexy drawl. His heart jolted.

"Deedra? Oh, God." Dropping the cane, he lurched forward, grasping her, fearing she'd disappear beneath his hands like so much smoke. But he gripped solid flesh. He yanked her to him, his arms circling her in a bear hug. It was her—not something conjured from his desperation and need. As proof, her heart slammed beneath his palm.

She was real.

Alive.

"I thought I'd lost you…like Callie… Oh, babe, where have you been?"

Deedra stiffened. He would never understand why she'd run away. Never believe that Mann had tried to kill her. He wasn't going to help. Coming here had been a mistake. Facing him, a bigger one. She tried squeezing a hand between them, tried shoving free from his embrace, but he held her tighter, as though needing to pull her into him, inside himself, as though releasing her would cause her to vanish.

Like Callie.

His mouth cut off her protest, taking hers in a kiss of hungry, possessive need. She'd forgotten the power of his touch, his kiss. How they could wipe out every other concern, no matter what else occurred in the rest of their lives. Her body leaned into his as if by its own will, all resistance melting. Her blood sang through her veins, slowly rousing need in the deepest part of her as if it were coming awake from a long hibernation. Flint sparked against flint, catching fire, flaring heat that chased the chill from her very soul.

He pulled back, his ragged breath caressing her lips. "Why?"

She flinched, finally wedging that hand between them, flattening it against his chest—his strong rock-hard chest—where she felt the thunderous thrum of his heart beneath her fingertips, each beat imbuing her with an awful guilt. He knew *why*. They'd grown so far apart emotionally she'd felt like a stranger in her own home. Alone in the battle against a mad killer. *I did what I had to do in order to survive.*

Beau eased back, still holding her tight, his gaze searching hers. "Why didn't you contact me?"

She glanced away, unwilling to see what her actions had done to him, not wanting to know.

He caught her chin and made her look at him. His raven eyebrows locked in a stormy scowl. And now she could see that investigator's mind of his churning, seeking explanations since she wasn't providing any. "Why did you cut and bleach your hair?"

"We need to talk." Her mouth was so dry the words seemed to stick on her tongue. "Can we go to the ranch?"

He was quiet for too long, his eyes darkening to a feral green. Wild cat eyes. Suspicious eyes. Interrogation eyes.

Damned detective eyes.

Deedra's stomach dipped toward her toes. The bouquet slipped from her hand. Vaguely she felt it brush her ankle, and she knew the petals were as crushed as the relationship she'd once had with this man. She braced for the force of his fury.

But Beau's words held more hurt than anger. "Had we really reached a point where you thought I wouldn't care if you were alive or dead?"

Chapter Two

Deedra could have stood his anger, could have taken his accusations, his disgust. But Beau Shanahan vulnerable was a thing she'd seen only once before.

The day he'd had to tell her their daughter...

She felt her every sense respond to this baring of his soul, this glimpse inside to the man she'd loved and never really reached. She swayed toward him, drawn by her lifelong need to be cherished and protected. The betrayal, the hurt, the crumbling of her dreams were forgotten in the possibilities of the moment.

But exposing his truest heart was apparently the one thing Beau could bear less than losing their child. The shutters dropped, and his expression hardened into the mask she'd seen far too often before she left. The face of the stranger who called himself her husband. The face of the detective obsessed with catching a cop killer.

The face of the daddy who blamed the mommy for the death of his beloved child.

He'd never said it. But she felt it every time he looked at her... as he was looking at her now.

Deedra's chest squeezed, and she took a step back from him, shrinking from the unspoken accusation, from the unrelenting guilt that she had not kept her child from harm. Her foot landed on something solid and round. A stick? The ground slipped out from under her.

Beau's strong hand grasped her wrist. Flesh on flesh, his on hers. Her heart began to hammer, her blood to heat. She recovered her balance as their gazes collided.

His detective eyes narrowed. "Why did you run away?"

She blew out a hard breath and tugged free of his grip, breaking the spell. "Someone was trying to kill me. You didn't want to believe it."

He stiffened as though she'd slapped him.

At the sound of voices, she glanced around. A couple was approaching a nearby grave. She lowered her voice. "Beau, please, this is hardly the place to discuss…this."

He cleared his throat, his own gaze slipping to the new arrivals. "I'll follow you back to the ranch."

Follow her. Cop tactics. Making sure she didn't run away…again.

Beau hopped back from her, bent at the waist and recovered the stick from beside her foot. A cane, she realized, as he leaned the bulk of his weight on it.

"Beau, what happened?"

He glanced sideways, then turned toward the car. "Not here."

He hobbled away from her. She started after him, but her foot crunched the bouquet and brought her up short. Deedra squatted and gathered crushed rose petals into her hand, then glanced at her daughter's pink head-stone, at the engraved lettering. Oddly, she felt nothing, and she realized she'd come to this cemetery expecting to feel…something. Heartache. Or anger. Or acceptance. Something that would allow her to let go. Some kind of release from the insane notion that her daughter still lived.

"Are you coming?" Beau called over his shoulder.

She jerked and gazed around at the couple who were now watching her. The Hermans, she realized, Arne and Kate. They owned the small spread next to the Shanahan land. They were eyeing Beau and her with curiosity. Buffalo Falls was a small and friendly town, and Beau hadn't even acknowledged his neighbors. They were likely wondering why. Wondering who *she* was.

She turned away before either of them got a good look at her face, placed what was left of the bouquet against the cold marble gravestone and hurried after Beau.

He had yet to reach his Jeep, hitching along with the gait of a man twice his age. But that was the only thing about him a woman might find unattractive. He had a sculpted backside that drew female glances wherever he went, shoulders as wide as a Montana sky, a waist whittled by hard work and the lean strong legs of a race horse.

Horse. Maybe he'd been kicked by one of their horses, she mused, pulling her gaze from Beau as she veered to her rental car. God knows, he spent as much time in the barn as he did in his cop car.

True to his words, he pulled up behind her and let her lead the way. She tried not to peer into the rearview mirror, but she felt his stare like a touch on her neck, down her spine, and the two-mile drive to the S bar S seemed hours long.

The familiar arched entrance rose from the hard-packed ground high and broad enough to accommodate a truck transporting a triple-wide mobile home. It had been carved from rough-hewn pine in Beau's great-grandfather's time and had withstood a good century's worth of broiling summer heat and paralyzing winter freeze. It would stand here long after she and Beau were gone.

The Shanahan land spread over nine hundred acres of rocky earth, scattered pine and rolling hillsides with the river winding through the farthest corner. The main house and outbuildings, barns and corrals were a half mile from the arch, visible in the distance. She slowed as they came into view and Beau shot past, his Jeep raising a plume of dust that sifted down over her vehicle.

But instead of heading for the ranch house, he veered into a side road that would eventually end at the hunting cabin out by the river. As though he'd communicated with her, Deedra understood at once and followed. There they could talk alone. If they went to the house or the barn, they risked running into his uncle Sean, who ran the ranch, or into Pilar, their housekeeper.

Both would ask too many questions.

Likely all the questions Beau wanted to ask.

She rubbed her lower back, absently stroking the pain, as she eased up on the gas pedal to avoid the worst of the dust. The cabin roof appeared on the horizon, and with its sighting came a slew of unbidden, taunting memories. She and Beau had usually ridden out here on horseback…to share a romantic picnic, a lovers' rendezvous.

Those times seemed so long in the past.

Light-years between now and then.

Beau drove faster, as if rushing to that happier time,

as if hurrying away from what their lives had become. But she could have told him running away wouldn't help or heal. Some things had to be faced head-on.

Life was not for cowards.

Deedra couldn't look away from the rough-hewn structure. The cabin hugged a ridge that sloped to the river, perched high enough to avoid the occasional flood, low enough to accommodate desired privacy. Built of logs and river rock, the single-story structure sported vaulted ceilings, a new steel roof and hardwood floors. A maintenance crew serviced it twice a month, dusting, cleaning, oiling the logs, keeping the freezer and pantry stocked with foodstuffs.

Here, as in town, the door was never locked. Trust thrived in this small corner of a world where barred windows and triple lock doors were the norm.

The irony that the trust between Beau and her had been broken here, of all places, wasn't lost on her.

Beau skidded to a stop and slammed out of the Jeep. He hobbled up the wide log steps, across the wrap-around porch and in through the massive door. She couldn't see his face, but she would bet his handsome features were twisted in pain, pain that cut clear to the bone.

The kind of pain no pill could buffer.

She'd thought the abuse and neglect she'd suffered during childhood had hardened her heart beyond reach, but first Beau, then Callie had cracked through the years-old armor and touched her in that most deep, most private place. She'd been so slow to trust, so cautious about casting off each tiny piece of that self-preserving shield and...so deliriously happy once she had.

Until Floyd Mann.

Something as cold and impenetrable as forged steel swept through her core, and Deedra felt her resolve calcify. She would never be vulnerable to anyone again.

She got out, took a deep breath of air so fresh and warm it ought to have exhumed the cold from the depths of her. Instead she shivered as though an icy breath grazed her neck. She shifted around and glanced at the surrounding hillsides. If someone had a rifle trained on her...

Her mouth dried. She scrambled onto the porch, the memory of the day she'd left giving speed to her feet, fear to her belly. She hustled through the door, shut it and leaned against it, her chest heaving as she struggled to catch her breath.

Beau stood at the fireplace, his formidable shoulders hunched, his attention on the crackling kindling, on the flames that licked through the dried scraps of wood, grabbing hold and flaring ever higher, scenting the room with pine. Another memory stirred within Deedra. Was he recalling it, too? The night they'd made love on that grizzly-skin rug, their passion as wild and fierce as the beast itself, their naked flesh as hot and hungry as the flames, their cries of ecstasy reaching into the rafters and filling the cabin with the sounds of joy and life.

The night of Callie's conception....

"Private." He cut through her thoughts. "To talk—"

"You don't need to explain," she interrupted.

He stared at the fire, his back to her as though he couldn't bear to look at her, whereas fifteen minutes ago he'd seemed unable to tear his gaze from her.

She stayed at the door, feeling safer away from the

windows, away from Beau, away from her own confused emotions. "I understand."

"I'm glad *you* do, because I don't understand any of this." Leaning on the cane, he dragged a hand through his thick hair, but still didn't look at her.

She wanted to pull him around, to make him face her, face this. But she stood frozen at the door, her own gaze bouncing, landing everywhere but on him.

Nothing had changed in this room, not the masculine decor of trophy heads and prize-winning trout that graced the walls, not the mission leather furniture the color of a buckskin pony, not the way the sun glinted off the river every afternoon to glare against the large picture window.

No, the room hadn't changed, *she* had. She no longer felt comfortable or welcomed here.

The scant space that separated them seemed Continental-Divide wide. Tension tugged her nerves so taut she feared they'd snap. "What happened to your leg?"

He turned then, avoiding her glance as if to avoid her question. His expression told her she wasn't going to like his answer. "I, er...was, ah...shot."

She blinked, shocked, though she knew she shouldn't be. A cop risked getting shot on a daily basis. A cop's wife lived with that fear. But somehow the reality was stunning. "How...who...?"

He glanced away, avoiding her gaze again.

And she knew. "Mann."

He wouldn't confirm it. But his silence made her certain. His face reddened, fury tightening his generous mouth into a thin white line. "I don't want to talk about Mann. I want you to tell me why the hell you ran? Why the hell you didn't let me know whether you were alive for two damned months?"

"Well, if you don't want to talk about Mann, then you don't want to hear why I left."

He swallowed hard, his big hands curling into fists, one at his side, one on the cane. A lock of his mussed hair brushed his forehead. His eyes were tired, weary in a way she'd never seen, full of pain and vulnerability and a darkness like thunderclouds roiling in the distance.

She felt the sudden urge for something strong and bracing to see her through the storm ahead. "You should probably get off that leg. I'll make some coffee."

"I'd rather have JD straight up."

Oh, yeah. Jack Daniels. Both strong and bracing. "Okay."

She went to the kitchen cabinet where the liquor was kept, pulled out two jelly glasses and filled each three fingers high. When she returned, Beau sat in one of two oversize chairs, his leg propped on the ottoman.

She handed him a glass, then sat on the chair facing his, on the edge of the deep cushion. He'd put a log on the fire before settling down. The heat felt good. The whiskey felt better, searing her middle and calming the butterflies in her stomach.

Deedra took a second swallow, then steadied her gaze on the face that had once made her heart sing, on the eyes that had once made her feel precious and pure, on the mouth that had once made her glad to be a woman.

How could it have gone so wrong? How could she have come to resent this man so much that she hadn't considered his feelings before doing what she'd done?

But she knew.

He was supposed to protect her. But he hadn't.

Couldn't or wouldn't. It didn't matter. He'd failed her when she'd needed him most.

She wasn't sure she could ever forgive him for that.

"The night I...left...I was coming back from Butte. The car behind moved into the oncoming lane, and then veered too close while passing me on Route 2, sideswiping me." She cringed, recalling the jarring bump of vehicle against vehicle, the awful sound of metal scraping metal. "You know how nervous I was about driving after the accident. This left me absolutely shaking. I stopped at the edge of the road to check the damage to my car. The other driver pulled over about twenty feet ahead. I figured he was going to exchange insurance information. The next thing I knew, he'd pulled out a rifle and was shooting at me. I dove back into my car and somehow managed to turn it back toward Butte."

"Did you get a look at the assailant?" *Assailant.* Cop word. He wore an unrelenting scowl. Likely recalling what the doctor had told him about her state of mind two months ago. Her fantasies. That, and Beau's need to be right—the need being his way of covering his fear.

"It was too dark, and I only realized later that the person had turned off the inside light of his car, because I couldn't see anything but the flashes of gunshot."

"You could have used your cell phone. Called nine one one. Called me."

As though *she* hadn't thought of that. As though she hadn't risked her life getting back into the car and taking off as fast as the car would go. She'd expected his disbelief, his lack of understanding, and yet it infuriated her. Damn it all. She'd done the right thing. Taken the only option left to her.

"I called your cell phone. Your pager. The ranch. Your office. The dispatch operator gave me the usual runaround, said you were 'unavailable.'" I deduced that to mean you were chasing a tip about Mann."

"I was." He shrugged, his whole demeanor defensive, unapologetic. "It was my job."

"Well, if I *could have* reached you, I'd have told you where to find him."

Beau gripped the jelly jar with white knuckles, but he wore a confident smirk. "He wasn't on Route 2 shooting at you."

"Wasn't he? Did you catch him that day? Did you find him wherever your 'source' told you he'd be?"

His smirk fled. "Well, no, but—"

Being right held no triumph for her. She took another hit of whiskey.

He said, "Why didn't you call nine one one?"

"What for?" She shook her head. "A temporary fix? Until the next time Mann ambushed me?"

"I would have kept you safe."

"You didn't. You weren't there. You were *never* there. I had no one but me. So I took myself out of the equation. Took off. Moved to a different state. Changed my name. My appearance."

"Without a thought as to how I'd take your disappearance coming so soon on the heels of losing Callie."

His words rang with bitterness, bringing back his earlier question: Had we really reached a point where you thought I wouldn't care if you were alive or dead? Maybe they had.

"I was physically ill, out of my mind with fear, so terrified of Mann, I *had* to disappear or die."

Beau finished his whiskey and clunked the drained glass onto the end table. "It was the cruelest, most selfish thing you could have done, Deedra."

If his glare pinned her, his words shamed her. She knew she didn't own all of the anguish and pain she saw in him. Okay, some of it belonged to her, but she hadn't meant to hurt Beau. Or had she? Had she been so hurt *by* him that she'd wanted, needed to hurt him back? Oh, God. She might have. "I'm sorry, Beau."

"Sorry? Sorry!" His eyes darkened to a green as cold as the dead of winter. "Sorry, my ass. You put me through hell. Where have you been? Hiding out with your old buddies?"

Deedra flinched. If he intended to bring up her past, she needed more whiskey.

"More?" she asked, gathering his glass.

"No." He caught hold of her wrist. The contact electrified the delicate skin there. He released her as though he'd felt the charge, too. "I've had enough."

"Well, I haven't." She hurried to the cupboard and refilled her glass. She walked back into the room and stood standing over him. "Freddie did help me... initially...but I haven't spoken with him since."

"Freddie," he spat the name. Beau hated the life he'd rescued her from. Hated Freddie Carter in particular.

But she owed Freddie more than she could ever repay, more than Beau would ever know. She'd run away from home at sixteen. Like so many other naive teens, she'd had no idea what life on the street held in store for lost children. Freddie Carter had saved her from a pimp. Shown her how to survive by using her wits instead of her body.

She'd kept ahead of the game most of the time, except when Beau had caught her stealing apples from that grocery store in Buffalo Falls and arrested her. Big cop. Tough cop. She'd had an attitude. He'd had a heart.

She'd forgotten his heart.

She gulped the whiskey.

Beau had shown her what it meant to be loved.

She'd forgotten that, too. She took a step toward him and felt herself sway. Booze and an empty stomach. Plus anemia. Not a good combination. She'd better sit down. She headed toward her chair. Her toe snagged the edge of the grizzly-bear rug. The next second she found herself airborne.

For a man with a bum leg, Beau reacted with a speed and grace he'd mastered as a boy catching and roping calves. He snatched her from disaster and tucked her gently onto his lap.

She wanted to stand, but the effort was suddenly too much for her. The world began to spin, growing blacker and blacker. Her head dipped to his shoulder, settling in the spot that had always seemed created for her.

The last thing she heard was Beau calling her name.

Chapter Three

The sniper crept down the slope toward the hunting cabin hefting a loaded, high-powered, long-range rifle. Grumbling, cursing. If Deedra hadn't spooked a while ago, she'd be lying next to that rental car in a pool of blood. The bitch had more lives than a cat.

Well, this time her luck and her lives had run out. She'd avoided this grim reaper for the last time. "I just need one clear shot."

Beneath the cruel sun, the sniper stole toward the gurgling river, hunched like a big-game hunter stalking prey, each step wary, each glance aimed at the huge picture window.

Though Deedra had seemed spooked earlier, the sniper felt sure that neither Shanahan had noticed the dirty, dented pickup following them from the cemetery. They'd been too caught up in their own drama to glance twice at a driver in a cowboy hat; hardly a remarkable sight in Buffalo Falls.

Figuring they were headed to the ranch house and that shooting Deedra would have to wait for another day, the sniper had almost turned back toward town. But their setting out for the cabin was pure destiny—opportunity blown in on the winds of fate.

Proof. The Universe agreed. Beau Shanahan had a lesson to learn. His actions had consequences. He had to hurt with an agony that only came with losing the things he most cherished.

Soon his suffering would be exquisite.

The sniper took quick furtive steps to a boulder balanced on the riverbank and squinted against the blinding sunlight that reflected off the wall of window. Damn. Better to view the prey through the scope.

The sniper lifted the rifle and peered into the lens.

Ah, there she was. Deedra. Lying on the sofa. Beau sat on the edge of the middle cushion, staring down at her supine body. His back to the sniper. Beau held her hands in both of his. So, he'd forgiven her for disappearing. For hiding from him.

Next step, make-up sex. A sweet loving reunion. A short, fatal uniting.

Smiling, the sniper stretched out on the boulder, hefted the rifle, then sighted the target. Deedra's chest filled the lens. There. The bull's-eye. That tiny area between her breasts caught in the crosshairs. That one clear shot.

Chapter Four

"Deedra?"

She opened her eyes, but the glare off the picture window at Beau's back had her slamming them shut again. Her head ached. Her stomach, too. A moment passed before she could squint up at him. Her focus cleared, and she read concern in his eyes.

"My God, Dee, what happened?" As though he'd been holding his breath, air rushed from between his sensual lips to feather her face.

She caught a hint of whiskey mixed with Beau's own scent, and a need deep inside her reached out to him. She wanted to taste that mouth, wanted him to bend down and take her in a mind-numbing, body-warming kiss that would wipe away all the fear.

"You aren't a woman who faints." He studied her face, seeking answers not intimacy. "Are you ill?"

"No, I...I haven't eaten much...today...and the whiskey..."

"That doesn't explain why your hands are so cold I can't warm them."

She realized only then that he held her hands between his large warm palms, rubbing them in a quick back-and-forth chafing motion, but no heat transferred from his flesh to hers, no blood found its way to her fingertips. She tried making light of it. "I might be a bit anemic."

"A bit?" His ebony brows dipped together as the reason dawned in his eyes. "You haven't had the surgery, have you?"

His voice rang with a tenderness she hadn't heard since…since what seemed like forever, and for a second or two she felt as though the chasm between them had narrowed to a distance both could span. She yearned to touch his cheek, graze her fingers down that fierce jaw, watch the green of his eyes slip from grass to jade, watch the concern melt to passion.

"You haven't had the surgery, have you?" he asked again.

"No." She tried to pull her hands free but hadn't the strength and instead settled deeper on the sofa. Then she frowned. How had he juggled her dead weight from the chair to the sofa with his leg injury? "It's one of the reasons I came ho—back."

"I don't understand."

"I know." A flashing glint from outside caught her eye. She glanced sharply at the picture window across from them, but sunlight, reflecting off the river, had turned the wide expanse of glass into something akin to a movie screen. She was presented a delightful vision of Beau's strong back and shoulders straining against the plaid of his western shirt.

A handsome cowboy bent over a damsel in distress.

She gazed at his beloved face again. His serious expression sent her mind shifting back to the events of the past couple of days, back to the reason she'd fled the Olympic Peninsula and hurried here.

She struggled up to her elbows. "I was going to have

the surgery. I made it as far as the operating room. But something happened. Something awful.''

''What?'' His jaw tensed, a sign of wariness she'd seen too often since they'd lost Callie.

The warm yearnings retreated, the sense she could bridge the gap between them collapsing in the next blink of her eyes. Was he going to listen? Really listen? And believe? Or would this be like every other time she'd tried to convince him that Mann meant to kill her?

The glint flashed from outside again. Deedra felt a sudden chill, a premonition, the same sensation she'd had while standing beside her car—as though she were being watched. Stalked. Targeted.

Her lethargic limbs lost all resistance, all weightiness. With a strength she could not guess the source of, she lurched up and knocked Beau in the chest with the heels of both hands. He swore, toppling over.

She hurled herself off the sofa and dropped onto him as a loud kaboom resounded from outside. The picture window exploded inward. Deedra buried a scream in Beau's chest as glass rained into the room.

Beau stopped struggling, caught her in a bear hug and set her behind him out of harm's way.

''Gotta get to the gun case,'' he whispered, scooting her back from the shattered window and shards of glass, ever farther from the sniper's aim. ''Keep low.''

He moved with stealth and grace as though he'd never suffered a gunshot to the leg. She moved with speed and zip as though she possessed energy to burn.

Another bullet blasted into the room. Wood paneling cracked. Deedra shrieked and scrambled to the kitchen. She pressed her back to a lower cabinet cupboard, an area blind to outsiders. She hugged her knees, her chest heaving with fear.

From her position she watched Beau activate the secret paneling beside the fireplace. He'd installed this secure spot to house ammunition and guns the week after Callie's birth. He wasn't taking any chances with his daughter's safety. *If only he'd been as cautious when Mann first turned his hatred on them,* she thought.

Beau pulled his favorite hunting rifle from the depths of the storage wall along with the Colt 45 he'd insisted she learn to shoot. Every gun in the hidden case was kept cleaned and loaded; natural predators—grizzlies, cougars, rattlers, and even coyotes—often wandered too near for safety.

This time the predator was human. She shivered at that fact.

Crouched low, Beau scrambled to her side.

"I've got to check the area beyond the window," he whispered. "See if our shooter is still out there."

She caught his wrist. "Beau, please be careful."

His gaze softened for a second. He squatted and thrust the Colt into her palm. "Keep that trained on the door, and do whatever you have to."

She nodded, and Beau scuttled off, disappearing back into the living room. Fear billowed in her chest as she hefted the Colt and pointed it at the door. *Beau would be all right. He was a cop. Trained to handle situations like this.*

Unlike Deedra.

She had street smarts aplenty, but none of her life experiences had prepared her to deal one-on-one with a cold-blooded killer. Oh, she could shoot. Accurately, too. In fact, if she'd had this gun the day Mann forced her car off the road there might have been a different outcome.

Beau, however, had decided she was too mentally unstrung to pack a deadly weapon. Too jumpy. He feared she'd accidentally shoot someone. Maybe Uncle Sean. Or Pilar. Or him.

Maybe herself.

She had to admit she'd given him reason to worry; on her worst days she *had* wanted to die. The loss of her child coupled with the tumor played havoc with her hormones, magnified her grief, her desperation and kept her on the brink of insanity. As long as the tumor remained inside her, she could not fully trust her mental state.

Nor should whoever wanted her dead. God help Mann if he should come through this door. She felt just *crazy* enough to show him that he wasn't the only one wanting revenge.

The muted crunch of glass sent her dark thoughts fleeing. Her heart thumped harder, louder, cutting off all other sounds. She willed herself to calm down and ignored the urge to check on Beau.

He counted on her, *needed her,* to watch his back.

She focused on that, pinning her gaze on the door, shaking her head and straining to make out any alien sounds from outside. After another unsettling crunch of breaking glass, an eerie silence fell over the house. Her mouth dried. She heard nothing from outside for several heart-stopping moments, and then she made out the clunk of a boot heel on one of the log porch steps.

Her hand tightened on the handle of the Colt. Her muscles bunched. A porch board creaked. Terror gathered in Deedra's throat, and a buzzing started in her ears. A solid footfall landed on the porch. Her breath snagged. Her finger feathered the trigger.

Oh, God, where was Beau? Had the sniper gotten him?

Another footstep.

Closer.

The buzzing in her ears grew louder.

Another step. Closer still.

The buzzing flared to a steady blare.

The sniper was at the door.

The knob turned.

Deedra braced the gun in both hands. The door swung open. Mann stood there. Taller than she remembered, the sunlight glaring around his frame, blurring his features. He was speaking, but she couldn't make out the words through the awful buzzing. She leveled the gun at his chest. "Don't come any closer."

He kept talking, but she couldn't hear. He set his rifle beside the door and stepped toward her, reaching for the Colt.

"Stay away from me!" she shouted.

He advanced on her.

Shoot. Shoot. But the message went no further than her brain. Her finger froze on the trigger.

He reached down, grabbed the Colt and lifted the barrel toward the ceiling. He wrenched the weapon from her. She cringed from him as horrified at what he might do to her now that he'd disarmed her as she was at her inability to protect herself. *Oh, Beau.* She'd let them both down. Mann lifted her by the shoulders and pulled her to her feet, dragging her to the door. The loud bang of it slamming shut hit her like a sobering slap.

Deedra shook her head. The buzzing receded, and

finally she began to make out words, a voice. Beau's voice. She blinked hard and went icy as she stared at the man holding her. Beau. Not Floyd Mann.

Her hands flew to her mouth but couldn't hold in the sob.

"Damn it all, woman, I thought you were going to kill me." He reached behind him and locked the door.

"Oh, my God, Beau. I saw...Mann...I..." Her voice trailed off in a singsong tone as though some inner horror kept flashing over her in waves, each pass presenting another gruesome scenario.

She touched his chest, her fingers tentative as if she sought assurance that he was real, just as he'd needed proof of her at the cemetery. As her touch grew stronger, bolder, she sobbed again. She fell into him, knocking him back against the door, her arms wrapping around his middle.

Beau gathered in her trembling body, bracing his weight on the door, his injured leg near buckling. His gaze scanned the area beyond the shattered window, a part of him alert to the danger that might still lurk beyond that now-vulnerable opening, but his healthy male body was slowly giving way to the awareness of woman pressed against the length of him.

Not just any woman.

Deedra.

He had thought he'd never hold her like this again, never feel her, smell her, touch her. Now he wanted to do all of that, and more: wanted to haul her down the hall to their bed, strip off their clothes and get lost in the frenzy of their lovemaking. The need throbbed through his veins, thickened his blood, his flesh.

He caught her face in his hands and, with a hunger too long denied, brought his mouth down on hers, taking possession of her lips, her tongue. Desire built to a sensuous drumbeat in his ears, blocking all sounds but the tiny, lusty whimpers of her compliance.

She ground her hips against his until his moans chorused hers in a song as old as time, a melodic promise that this most intimate joining would heal the way to their reunion. That if this were right, then surely everything else could be made right.

He bent to lift her into his arms, and she came eagerly, their lips locked, the connection too strong to break. He gathered her body to his chest, and his leg gave out. He startled, tried catching himself. Deedra yelped. They collapsed to the floor in a tangle of limbs. Her cheeks were flushed with desire, her eyes glazed with unfulfilled want. Then a smirk curved her sexy mouth, and Beau started to laugh.

A large chunk of picture window dropped from the pane. The crash shattered the moment and the closeness. Beau sobered, berating himself for needing her so much he'd forgotten, even for a heartbeat, the danger that lurked outside.

Or the danger that lurked inside. The emotional danger.

God, was he crazy? How could he think making love would bridge the chasm in their relationship? Had he learned nothing from the time after Callie's disappearance? If sex were a cure-all, he wouldn't have fled the intimacy of their marriage bed and driven Deedra to a point where she'd rather hide than be with him. He struggled to his feet, allowing her to help him up, gazing into her gorgeous gray eyes.

In that second he realized he'd had a narrow escape. It would hurt him more than he could bear if he had Deedra again and then she chose to walk out once more.

Better not to have her at all.

"We need to call in some backup." He gathered his cane from the floor and hobbled to the wall phone in the kitchen.

"Did you see anyone out there?" Deedra followed him but held back, hugging herself, her gaze not quite meeting his. She seemed ill at ease as though she regretted their intimacy, their kiss. As though she were shocked at what had almost happened between them, unhappy that she'd wanted it as much as he.

"No, I didn't see anyone." Beau blew out a hard breath and lifted the receiver. At least the sniper hadn't cut the phone line. He dialed the ranch. "There were some cartridge shells near that big boulder by the river, but the ground is too dry for footprints. Too rocky. I didn't even spot any sign of a vehicle heading away down the road."

As soon as his uncle answered, he said, "Sean, there's been some trouble out at the cabin. Get hold of Heck Long, tell him and Nora Lee to get out here ASAP, and then send out a couple of the barn hands and a load of planking. The main window needs to be boarded up until it can be replaced. I'll explain later. Oh, and tell Pilar to set an extra plate for supper tonight."

He hung up to find Deedra standing against the counter, her face chalky, her eyes narrowed accusingly. "You didn't tell Sean about Mann. Why? Don't tell me you actually think it was some hunter? Or...or a poacher?"

"No, I don't think that." He stood stock-still, not knowing how to approach her, how to bridge that unbridgeable gap. She appeared small and fragile, but at her core there was a strength built from years surviving by her wits. She didn't cry or brood or fall apart like other women. He supposed that was why he'd felt so helpless when she *had* fallen apart after losing Callie.

He said, "An accidental first shot wouldn't explain the second. That was deliberate. Whoever it was, was firing at us."

"Mann," she whispered.

"Maybe." He motioned her toward the round dining table. "We've got some time before the men and Nora Lee show up. I think you'd better tell me exactly what happened at that hospital in Washington State."

Deedra closed the blinds over the nook window and sat. Beau prepared a plate of crackers and cheese before joining her. "Eat. I don't want you fainting again."

She did as directed, explaining between bites. "I had gone to the hospital weeks in advance of the hysterectomy to have my blood stored. Day before yesterday I arrived early, was prepped, wheeled into the operating room and given anesthesia. So when I awakened in recovery, I naturally assumed I'd had the procedure."

"But you hadn't."

"No. As I was coming around I heard two nurses talking about another patient." She grimaced, recalling. "A woman who hadn't made it through her own surgery, and, oh, Beau, I felt so bad for her, so awful for her family. But I was relieved, grateful, so damned glad that the same fate hadn't been mine. Only, for once, it was more than survival instinct. I know it sounds strange, but it was as if someone had turned on the colors again, as if I'd been reborn."

She met his eyes then, and he realized she meant

what she said, that she might actually, finally have begun healing.

"But with that revelation came another. A terrifying one." She chewed a cracker with cheese, seeming to need the momentary distance between herself and the horror. "The dead woman had been given the wrong blood. The wrong blood type."

Beau swore. "Good God, how could anyone make that kind of a mistake?"

"The mistake cost Mrs. Orowitz her life. But the tragedy was nearly twofold. Her blood had been switched with another surgery patient's."

"Yours?" His eyebrows lifted.

"Yes."

"What kind of malpractice mansion were you in?"

"It was no foul-up, Beau. The nurse said it was done on purpose and if the anesthesiologist hadn't realized it, I would have been dead, too. I knew then that Mann had found me. That he'd almost killed me again. That he had killed an innocent woman."

"You think Mann did this?"

"Of course it was Mann. I can't fight him alone," she implored. "Please, Beau, I need your help. Will you help me?"

But he was a mental beat behind her. "How could it be Mann? According to you, no one knew where you went. So, how can you expect me to believe that Mann found you in another state? That he somehow discovered where you were having surgery, somehow gained access to where they kept the blood and switched it?"

"I...I don't know." Her expression clouded. She actually seemed not to have considered this.

"Well, there has to be some explanation and the obvious one is that somebody knew where you were."

"No..." Her frown deepened.

Beau tilted his head. "Not even your old pal Freddie?"

She stiffened, and he could see he'd hit the ball out of the park. She shook her head. "No...Freddie wouldn't..."

"Freddie would."

"No—"

"Oh, hell, Dee. Freddie Carter would sell his grandmother for a bottle of booze."

She blanched. Her face going ashen.

He covered her cold hand. He knew how this had to hurt. She preferred remembering the Freddie who'd rescued her from the mean streets of Butte, who'd taken her in and taught her how to survive without selling her body. But Freddie liked whiskey. In recent years, he liked whiskey more than he liked anything. "I'm sorry, babe."

The loud rattle of a loose muffler brought Beau to his feet, to the window over the sink. Relief swept through him at the sight of the familiar black-and-white Cherokee pulling up out front. "It's Heck. By the way, I'm not a state trooper anymore. I'm the new sheriff of Buffalo Falls. Heck's my deputy."

Her gray eyes widened.

He said, "Stay here. I want to give him the facts without his being distracted by your resurrection."

He stepped out onto the porch. Heck, medium height with a wiry build, a military haircut and small brown eyes, spilled from the patrol car. He was alone. "Where's Nora Lee?"

"Was on patrol. She's heading in to man the office

while we're out here.'' Before Beau could respond, Heck added, ''I've been tryin' to reach you ever-where, Sheriff. They caught Floyd Mann this mornin'. Got him in a jail cell in Butte.''

Chapter Five

Floyd Mann, captured outside his mountain cabin. That morning. Imprisoned in Butte. That morning. Not Mann down by the river. Shooting at them. Trying to kill them.

Deedra felt empty and confused, as though a long-held truth had been ripped from her mind, her heart, the threads that had held it in place dangling like torn puppet strings. Someone was playing her. Had been all along.

The fact stunned her as much as her being here with Beau had stunned first Heck Long and then the S bar S ranch hands who'd arrived in his wake. For a while mass chaos had prevailed. The men had seemed incapable of deciding which floored them more, the boss's wife's return or the sniper's assault.

Beau had directed them to gather evidence, clean up the mess and secure the cabin. Then he'd caught Deedra by the arm and guided her outside and into his car. The question she couldn't bring herself to ask aloud sat between them like a glass wall.

If not Mann, who? Who wanted to kill her?

Beau wore a scowl, and she could almost hear his mind churning, likely mulling this same question. But he didn't speak, and the silence grew with every mile, glass wall thickening, an invisible wedge shoving them further apart.

Deedra sank low, cringing in on herself, terrified that whoever had shot at them earlier might try again as they drove to Butte. Her nervous hands clutched the edge of the seat. Her fingertips brushed paper, something tucked between the door and floorboards, as though it had slipped off the cushion. She grasped it. Nothing official. Just a card-shaped envelope addressed to Beau in a woman's flowery script. The *E* curlicued.

She glanced at Beau, but his concentration remained on the road, not on what she was doing. She looked again at the envelope, deciding it was nothing important or he wouldn't have been careless enough to misplace it. She set it on the seat between them, saw it might slip through the cushions and stuffed it into her pocket.

Beau exited the highway for the outskirts of Butte.

The increase in traffic shattered Deedra's fragile sense of security. The hair on her neck rose, her palms grew damp. She cast her gaze in all directions, searching for the sniper and his rifle.

Nerves filled her throat each time the car slowed or came to a standstill at a stoplight or intersection. Suddenly everyone was suspect. She cast sidelong glances at each vehicle, at each motorist—old men, teenage boys, young mothers, and middle-aged matrons.

If not Mann, then who? Who would pull out a gun and fire at them?

THE AIR in the Butte cop shop felt electric. They'd caught the lowest of the low. Let the celebration begin. Beau was surprised he didn't share the elation.

After ushering Deedra into the cubicle behind the one-way mirror, Beau stood outside the interview room with Captain Parker. He clenched and unclenched his hands, unaware of the reflexive action.

"I know you'd like five minutes alone with him, Shanahan." Parker eyed his fisted hands. "We all would."

"He didn't shoot *your* deputy," Beau growled, narrowing his gaze.

"No. But he's my collar." Parker had rough-hewn features that had always called to mind those bears carved from logs with chain saws. For all his coarse exterior, Parker spoke with the dulcet tones of a ballad singer. Something that made him sound deceptively harmless. "If you lay one finger on him, I'll yank your ass out of there. Understand?"

"Yeah, yeah."

"I mean it, Shanahan. We need this conviction clean. No lawyers crying police brutality."

"The verdict is a foregone conclusion."

Parker's expression darkened. "Not necessarily. He could have the sympathy of some jurors. We're being pressured from all sides about the kind of pursuit that killed his pregnant wife."

Beau winced, hating that he shared the pain of losing a child with a scumbag like Mann, hating that in some small part of his soul he held a modicum of sympathy for him. The former white supremacist had murdered one of Beau's best deputies, Doug Mallory. Killed him in cold blood.

Doug Mallory had kids, too.

His face tightened.

Parker scowled. "If the only reason you're here is to vent your spleen, I won't let you see him."

Once, he'd wanted Mann dead. As dead as Mallory. As dead as his daughter.

Beau shook himself. How the tables had turned. Last time he'd faced Mann, he'd expected the cop killer would put an end to his misery. Beau hadn't even tried to protect himself. He hadn't pulled his trigger. He'd just wanted to die.

It had all changed twice more since then.

A week ago, yesterday, even this morning, Beau would have gladly smashed Mann's face. For Deedra. For Callie. For his lower leg. But Mann hadn't murdered Deedra, hadn't been trying to. Probably had had nothing to do with Callie. And his leg injury was his own damned fault.

Parker slapped a hand on his shoulder. "What do you say? Can you control that famous Irish temper?"

Beau stared into the other cop's eyes and felt a sudden sense of being rudderless. He'd been heading one direction, full speed ahead, then without warning the wind had left his sails and the gas had drained from his tank. He'd come to a standstill with no idea how to start again or in which direction to set out.

He had only enough sense to realize violence wouldn't get his motors revved, but he did need confirmation and to lay to rest any lingering doubts in Deedra's mind that Mann had had anything to do with her terror, with losing Callie. "I won't touch a pore on his bald head. I just want to ask him a few questions."

DEEDRA'S STOMACH BURNED as she stared through the one-way mirror at the spook who'd haunted her days and nights for far too long. Floyd Mann. Built like an ogre in a fairy tale, he hunched in a metal chair across the table from Beau. Defiance rose off him like a bad odor.

He'd shaved his helmet-size head, preferring swastika tattoos in place of hair, the blue ink black against his buttermilk-pale skin. The letters K-I-L-L-C-O-P-S etched the flesh above his knuckles. His ankles wore shackles, his face a sneer.

"How's the leg, Shanahan?" he asked on a mocking laugh. Then, as though sensing they were not alone, he raised his gaze to the mirror, watery blue eyes sweeping over its surface. He grinned. Cocky. A man who used attitude in the face of authority. In the face of fear? Would such an unlawful man tell Beau, a cop, the truth?

Deedra clutched her hands in her lap. What was the truth? Had Mann ever tried to kill her? Did he even know anything about Callie?

Beau said, "If I were you, Mann, I'd be more concerned about my own hide. Look where you've landed."

"Mallory deserved to die." The cockiness fled from Mann's face and sorrow trembled through his voice. "He killed Merry Sue and our unborn kid."

"It was an accident." Beau spoke so low she barely caught the words.

"T'was a car chase after a two-bit felon. Mallory shoulda let the guy go for another day. He cost me my family and all he had to offer was apologies. Like that excused what he done. Like that could bring back my Merry Sue."

Beau lowered his head. He looked shaken when he lifted it again, as though he understood this man's pain. "Is that why you came after my wife and my baby?"

Deedra leaned to the edge of her chair, heart racing.

Mann shook his head. "What you talkin' about? I never went after yer missus or yer kid. I wouldn't take no other man's family the way mine was took from me."

"No. You just came after me. The Jeep you rigged to hurt me caused the accident my wife and daughter had. We lost our child just as though you'd snatched her away."

"I never come after you, Shanahan. Never. I swear it on my sweet Merry Sue's grave."

"But the Jeep?"

"Not my doin'." Mann shook his head.

Beau tapped his wounded leg. "You tried to kill me."

"Hell, I did. I woulda never shot you, 'cept you was 'bout to shoot me. I didn't kill ya. But I coulda if I'd wanted. Hell, I can down a coon outta a tree top by hittin' him dead in the left eyeball. If'n I wanted you dead, Shanahan, I'd a blowed yer pretty face clean away. Why you think I aimed for your leg?" He shook his head. "Uh, uh. *I* ain't the one after you."

Mann lifted his watery gaze to the mirror again, his stare intent as though he could see Deedra, as though he were talking to Deedra. "Not me."

DEEDRA SAT in the cubicle behind the one-way mirror long after the others left, long after Mann was taken away. She felt as empty as the room she faced. Alone. Shaken. No longer grasping at a single shred of hope that the hell in her life could be resolved with Mann's capture.

Tears for all she'd lost stung her eyes. She swiped at them. Furious that her hands came away damp. Crying was for weak females, like her mother. She was nothing like her mother. She didn't let men abuse her. She didn't cry and wish things were different. She acted. She caused change.

She'd done it at sixteen. She'd done it two months ago. She'd do it now.

She shoved her hand into her pocket for a hankie. She found paper, but not a tissue. *The envelope from beneath the seat in Beau's car*. She stared at the flowery feminine scrawl, sniffing back the residue of tears. She shouldn't open this, shouldn't read it. Deedra laughed at the ridiculous thought. When had what she shouldn't do ever stopped her? She pulled the sheet of paper from its sheath.

The note was written in the same frothy penmanship as the envelope.

Beau, darling,
Just the thought of last
night, of you in my bed,
has me hot and anxious
for tonight. Don't be
late, lover. I have a
naughty new treat for you.
　　Love, me

It was decorated with tiny hearts and a lipstick smudge like a kiss.

Deedra's stomach pitched, and nausea rose up her throat. For all that was wrong with their marriage, she had never suspected Beau of infidelity. Had she been a fool? Had she, who prided herself on street smarts, on cynicism, actually been gullible in this one area?

It would sure explain why he'd stayed out of their bed the months before she'd gone underground.

She gripped the note with white knuckles, choking on a sharp, searing fury. *Damn it, Beau.* He hadn't been there when she'd needed him most. Was it because he'd been getting what he needed from some other woman?

Beau opened the door, startling her. "We'd better go."

"Sure." Deedra crammed the note and envelope into her pocket, struggling to still the tremors racking her insides. She squelched the urge to confront him here and now as she'd squelched the urge to cry. This was not the place for either. But as much as she thought herself in control, she found her legs wobbly, her movements jerky. Her lower back ached with renewed agony.

In all the excitement of running into Beau, being nearly shot and confronting Mann, she'd forgotten for a while her health problem. But like an ugly rumor, it would come back to haunt her until she put it right.

It seemed she had several things to put right in her life.

Beau sheltered her like a child until she was inside the car. *My own personal bodyguard.* Instead of reassuring her, his demeanor reawakened her fear of the shooter. She forgot all about the love note, about his possible infidelity, about crying, about the pain in her lower back, in lieu of staying alive.

She shrank into her seat, wanting to disappear. Become invisible. Wanting Mann to be guilty. "Was Mann lying?"

Beau shook his head. A lock of his black hair fell onto his forehead and in that moment he looked so like Callie her heart sputtered.

He said, "Facts back up a couple of points of his

story. He wasn't shooting at us at the hunting lodge earlier today.''

''And…?''

Beau scowled. ''He *could* have killed me instead of shooting me in the leg.''

Deedra blinked in surprise. Beau was a crack shot. As good as Mann claimed to be. The former white supremacist couldn't have outgunned Beau without Beau somehow permitting it, but her husband offered no enlightenment.

Hell, what did it matter? She hugged herself. Mann hadn't taken her little girl. He hadn't done any of this. ''If Mann didn't cut the brake line on the Jeep, who did? Who wants me dead, Beau?''

He frowned. ''Those shots today could have been for either of us.''

''No.'' She cast a watchful eye for the sniper. ''You've been here all along. You haven't been hiding or taking any kind of precautions. If you were the target, whoever it is would have come after you before today.''

He seemed to see her point. ''And whoever it is *did* come after *you* in Washington.''

''Exactly. Why *me?*'' Why wasn't it enough that Callie had been taken from them? Why did someone want *her* out of Beau's life, too? She hugged herself tighter and recalled the note in her pocket. Who had written it? Did it have anything to do with all of this? Was some woman trying to kill her in order to have Beau to herself?

''Who, Beau?'' She pulled the note from her pocket and shook it at him. ''Her?''

Beau looked startled. His eyes turned dark, a green that was almost black. Even scowling, he had the kind of appeal that spoke to the basic core of a woman. She'd felt it the moment of their first encounter. She felt it now. He oozed confidence. Power. Danger. All things that touched her in some secret place. That tugged her toward him with a magnetic pull. Surely it touched other women, too.

"What the hell is that?" Beau snatched the paper from her and scanned it. His face went thunderous. He cursed and crushed the love note. "Where did you get this?"

"Under this seat. Pretty careless of you."

"I wasn't trying to hide it. This is from some deluded woman who thinks she and I are having an affair."

"What do you mean she *thinks* you're having an affair? She sounds pretty damned sure about it to me."

"A complete fantasy. *Her* fantasy. Dee, I've never met this—this nutcase."

"Haven't you?"

"No." He caught her chin in his hand, his hold gentle but firm. He made her look at him. His eyes had lightened to jade. "I've done a lot of things wrong this past year, but *that* is one line I never crossed. I never cheated on you."

When he looked at her like this the ice melted from her heart. The hurt and the anger dissolved and floated off like excess air. Oh, how she wanted to believe him, wanted to fold herself against his chest, listen to his heart beat until it matched the rhythm of her own. Oh, how she wanted to trust him and let him keep her safe.

But he hadn't kept her safe. Couldn't keep her safe.

She pulled free from his grasp. Wounded at his denial. Offended. Indignant. Hurt as she'd never been by this man and that was saying a lot. "Most men deny infidelity when confronted with proof of it."

He growled low in his throat, started the car and stomped on the gas. Deedra snapped back against the seat. How many of their disagreements had ended exactly like this? She pitched a fit. He clammed up.

Damn him. Someone—probably his mistress—wanted her dead, and all he cared about was keeping his infidelity a secret. She sank lower in the seat, fear squeezing her. Worse than before. Earlier she'd felt she had Beau on her side. Now she was truly alone. As alone as she'd been in Washington state.

The car wended through town, and she realized they weren't headed to the outskirts of Butte, but rather to a seedy downtown area. She glanced at Beau. He still wore a scowl, but she doubted he felt more angry than she did. "Where are we going?"

He didn't look at her. "To find out who's trying to kill you."

To his girlfriend's? "We're just going to show up and confront her?"

"Her?" He made a face as though she'd said the sun was a hairy black ball. Then, realizing who she meant, he shook his head and swore. "There is no *her*. We're going to track down your buddy, Freddie Carter. He sold you out. He knows who is trying to kill you."

Chapter Six

"Freddie?" She started to argue, heard the protest in her voice, felt it along the hair on her neck. But she could no longer deny the validity of Beau's suspicions. Damn it all. She did not want to believe he was right about her old friend, but Freddie *was* the only one who knew where she was going when she ran away. He'd helped her procure fake ID. Knew the name she'd been using. Knew where she had settled.

How else could the killer have found her, if not through Freddie?

Her heart ached at the thought.

This had been some day. Within hours she'd discovered the only two men she'd ever trusted in her life had both betrayed her. She didn't want to believe it of either of them.

She used to not be naive.

But then, Freddie used to hate drinking and drunks.

"Where is he likely to be?"

"Any one of a dozen places." Deedra shrugged. "The best thing to do is ask his mother."

"His mother?" Beau glanced at her in surprise. "I thought he was another orphan of the streets. What did he do, reconnect with his family after he grew up?"

"With his mother. Freddie moved out of the house at seventeen after beating his alcoholic father nearly to death. His old man died a year later of alcohol poisoning, and though Freddie didn't move back in, he's tight with Nell. He gives her money when he can and occasionally crashes there overnight, if he hasn't got somewhere else to sleep. She could know what he's doing this week, and if so, that will give me some idea where we might find him."

"Where does she live?"

She rattled off the address. Nell Carter's house was in an older neighborhood on the outskirts of Butte. Painted a sunny yellow with electric-blue trim, the trilevel sat on a corner lot, surrounded by fenced front and backyards. An array of gaily colored plastic toys littered the grass and walkway.

"She runs a day care," Deedra explained.

"Oh, yeah? Where are the kids?" Beau pulled the car to the curb. "Place looks deserted—abandoned—as if everyone left in the middle of playing."

"Maybe it's naptime." She suggested, frowning as she regarded the house. "The curtains are all drawn."

"Kind of late for naps." Beau opened his door. "This time of day parents ought to be arriving from work to pick up their kids."

"That is odd." Deedra got out of the car.

Beau said, "Maybe the city got smart and shut her down."

"Don't tar Nell with the same brush you use on Freddie. She doesn't drink, doesn't allow Freddie here if he's been drinking. She hates drunks as much as her son used to."

Beau grumbled something under his breath, but the only word she caught was "losers."

Deedra bristled. ''Nell's not a loser. She's a great day-care provider.''

''Yeah, whatever.''

She shook her head, wanting to shake him. He hated her past, found every opportunity to put it down. As if she could change it. As if it hadn't shaped her into the woman she'd become. A woman she *thought* he'd fallen in love with, warts and all. But maybe this was why they hadn't been able to make it when the chips were down. Maybe their backgrounds were just too different, too much to surmount over the long haul.

With that sad thought, she unlatched the gate. She stepped into the yard but pulled up short. Her gaze had locked on a tiny red wagon lying on its side, a stuffed bunny sprawled in the dirt beside it. In her mind's eye, Deedra saw the police photographs of her accident.

She didn't recall the accident. Her doctor said the memory loss was likely caused by the blow she'd taken to the head. She'd been all but dead when they'd found her. Apparently she'd been using the shortcut through wooded acreage at the back of the ranch, a winding dirt road. The brakes had given out on a sharp curve. She'd rounded the corner on two wheels and slammed into a fallen tree. Her head impacted with the windshield, and a branch had stabbed her very near her heart. When she'd been discovered, dusk had fallen over the woods.

The Jeep had lain on its side, the baby seat empty, Callie's favorite stuffed bunny sprawled in the dirt road.

Callie knew exactly how to release the button on her car seat. The consensus of opinion held that she'd freed herself, climbed out of the Jeep and toddled off into the woods. But no sign of her had ever been found, and Deedra had taken that as proof that her daughter was still alive.

Proof that Floyd Mann had abducted her.

But that wasn't the case, and now she had to face reality. An eighteen-month-old child could not have survived in those woods for more than a few hours. Certainly not days. Certainly not this long.

"What's the matter?" Beau reached for her, but she shook herself and stumbled back.

"Nothing. I'm sorry." She forced the painful musings away and made herself move. Giving the wagon a wide berth, she hurried up to the porch. There was no sound inside. No children's voices, no television, no radio. Just silence. Concern for Nell swept her. Had she gotten sick or something?

Beau joined her on the porch and rang the bell.

"It doesn't work. Freddie disconnected it so it wouldn't disturb the kids during naptime."

"Well, if any are napping now, they won't be for long." He knocked. The silence seemed louder with every bang of his fist against the wood. At length he said, "She's not home. I'm going to try and call her on the cell phone."

They returned to the car, and while Beau dialed the number written on the day-care sign and listened, Deedra studied the house. It did have the appearance of activity abruptly ceased.

"She's not answering her phone, either. You'd think, running a business, she'd have an answering machine."

"She does."

"It's not on."

"This is just so unlike Nell. I'm concerned, Beau."

Deedra glanced at the split-entry next door. "Maybe we should ask one of the neighbors."

"Oh, no you don't." Beau started the engine. "We've got some mad sniper following us around. We're perfect targets on this street."

He pulled away from the curb.

Deedra gave the house one last glance. A movement at the second-floor window caught her eye. A curtain? Or sun glaring off the glass looking like movement?

Beau said, "How did you contact him last time?"

"I called around. Found him at a hole in the wall called The Copper Spittoon."

"That's way over in the industrial area."

"Yes, it is."

He pulled a U-turn.

"Beau, there's no guarantee he'll be there today. He could be at any one of a dozen dives."

"It's a starting point."

Deedra shoved her hands though her short blond hair. In the old days, Freddie and she had hustled guests at the bigger hotels. If they were lucky, they'd end up with enough pocket money to buy a thick steak and a good bottle of wine. Sometimes they'd scammed enough to actually stay in one of the suites for a week or two. But after she "went straight," as Freddie called it, he seemed to lose all interest in the hustle. She'd never been sure of the reason. Age. Change. Life.

Her leaving?

"You see his car here?" Beau asked, pulling between the vehicles parked outside the bar.

She cast a cautious glance at the few cars around them and shook her head. "I don't know what he's driving these days."

Beau opened his door, eyeing the building with disdain. "Freddie used to cater to a better class of dive."

There was no denying how far Freddie had fallen.

The Copper Spittoon, as tarnished a watering hole as ever existed, squatted between two abandoned industrial warehouses, the only sign of life on an otherwise dead street. Deedra stepped warily from the car. There was a brownish-red stain on the road as though someone had recently run down a stray dog or coyote, splattering it across the pavement.

She shook off the ugly thought and gave her attention to the bar. Nothing had changed since she'd last seen it. The filthy windows obscured the interior. A single neon sign hung over the door, winking and buzzing like some aging hooker making crude come-ons to leery customers.

The inside stank of cigarettes, spilled booze and forsaken hopes. A country ballad—circa Hank Williams, Sr.,—whispered on the air. Something crunched beneath her feet. Peanut shells that she'd bet had been there since the doors first opened.

Three men hugged bar stools, their heads lost in a haze of smoke. Regulars. None of them Freddie. Beau stepped up to them. "Any of you know Freddie Carter?"

Six bloodshot eyes turned toward him. The old man on the end squinted at Beau. "Who'd you say?"

"Freddie Carter. Six foot. Skinny as a post. Dirty-blond hair. Thick brown beard."

"Oh, sure, Freddie." The old man's head bobbed, then he eyed Beau more closely. "You a cop, ain't ya."

Beau nodded.

The other two men shifted back to their respective drinks on hearing Beau was police.

But the old man just squinted harder, glancing at Deedra. "She ain't no cop, though."

"No," she agreed. "I'm not."

He focused his attention back to Beau. "Freddie done somethin' wrong?"

"Not that I know of. My business with him is strictly personal."

The old man raised a disbelieving eyebrow and reached for his beer. "Well, I ain't seen him in a week or so now. You might try The Pit. He hangs there off and on."

Beau clapped him on the shoulder and laid a twenty next to the man's icy mug. "Are you sure you haven't seen him? This is real important."

The man's gnarled fingers snatched up the money and he stuffed the bill into his pants pocket. "I still don't know where he is. I ain't seen hide nor hair of him in a week. Say, now, come to think of it, that's kind of strange. Wonder where he is?"

"Probably hiding from me," Beau whispered to Deedra. "Knows I'll skin him for siccing a killer on you."

Deedra spied a man near a booth in the back, leaning down, talking to someone she couldn't see. She tugged Beau's sleeve and directed his gaze. "That bartender was on duty the day I met Freddie here."

Beau and the bartender exchanged names, but all Deedra caught of the other man's was "Wolf."

Wolf stood all of five-seven with a shaved head and bulging muscles beneath a skintight T-shirt. His smile showed big, white canine teeth. He exuded nervous energy, giving Deedra the impression that he might pounce at any moment. Reflexively she inched closer to Beau.

"You know Freddie Carter?"

The question widened the bartender's eyes. He studied Beau a long moment. "I've already told the cops everything I know."

Beau stiffened. "What are you talking about?"

"Aren't you following up on the case?"

"So, there's a case of some kind." Beau gazed at Deedra as if to say, "It figures. Freddie is probably in jail even as we stand here."

Her stomach pinched at the thought of Freddie getting caught and facing serious jail time. She asked, "What did Freddie do?"

"What did he…?" Wolf gave a sarcastic laugh and glanced at the women seated in the booth. "It wasn't what he did, it's what was done to him."

"It was awful," the brunette said, making a disgusted face.

"I got sick," added her blond companion. "Threw up all over my best shoes."

"What?" Deedra's pulse skipped, alarm speeding through her veins. "What happened to him?"

Wolf turned a steely gaze on her. "Hit and run. Right out front."

"I saw the whole thing," the brunette said. "We were just standing out there talking when that big dark van came roaring straight at us. Freddie pushed me aside, but couldn't get out of the way quick enough. He saved my life. Took the hit for me."

"Oh, there was blood everywhere." The blonde moaned, slapping her hand over her mouth.

"I knew that van. Told the cops it belonged to one

of my regulars. 'Course later we found out it was stolen."

Deedra thought of the reddish-brown stain on the road out front and felt sick, frantic. "Where did they take him? Which hospital?"

"No hospital," the blonde answered.

"Where?" Beau demanded, gripping Deedra by both arms, keeping her upright.

"The morgue," Wolf said. "He was road kill. Flattened like a garbage rat."

"No!" Deedra screamed as the walls seemed to rush at her, the room starting to shrink, to fill with a thick black fog. Oh, God, she was going to faint for the second time in one day. No. She fought the sensation as she felt Beau's arms enfold her.

He moved her to a table and pressed her into a chair. He barked at the bartender, "Get some brandy! Quick!"

Wolf was back with it in seconds.

"Sip it slow," Beau advised, tipping the shot glass toward her mouth.

Deedra sipped. The liquor burned down her throat, seared through her blood and awakened her numbed nerves. No wonder Nell's house looked like life interrupted. No wonder all the drapes were drawn against the outside world. Freddie was dead. Murdered. She couldn't process it. Couldn't. Wouldn't. Not here. She took another few sips, then gestured Beau closer. He bent over and leaned toward her. She murmured, "Take me out of here."

"Are you sure?"

She met his gaze, but could only nod.

"Think you can stand?"

She nodded again.

"And walk?"

She blew out a frustrated breath. Why did he always have to question everything? She struggled to stand. "I'm okay."

He helped her to her feet. She swayed slightly. No. She was not going to fall apart. Not going to cry here. Not going to grieve for Freddie in a room full of strangers. She dug deep into herself, gathered as much poise as she could muster and started for the door.

All of the patrons had stopped drinking and chatting. Their gazes were glued to Beau and her as he held her to him and guided her outside. Just as the door shut, she heard the old man ask, "What got her so upset?"

The bright sunlight blinded Deedra. She blinked hard against the glare. Hard against a sting of tears. The street was as quiet and deserted as when they'd arrived. The buzz of the neon sign made the only noise. Deedra held her gaze high, unwilling to look at the rusty stains, but she couldn't erase the image from her mind. Not some animal's blood. Freddie's blood.

Her knees wobbled, and she struggled to stay erect. Beau seemed not to notice, and as she started to sink toward the ground, she pulled him with her. A gunshot resounded from somewhere nearby. Overhead, the neon sign hissed and sparked, then went as dead as Freddie.

The second shot found Deedra on the pavement, her blood mixing with that of her old friend's.

Chapter Seven

Over the crack of the second shot, Deedra heard Beau shout, "Get down!"

He slammed into her. Knocked her off her feet. She saw the ground rushing to meet her. She yelped and threw her hands out to buffer the impact. Skin scraped from her palms and knees. Blood sprang in the wounds. Oddly, she felt no pain, just a grinding slowness as though something had cranked the movement of time to a crawl. Her vision narrowed. Her attention snagged on the drips of her blood falling on the spot where Freddie had died, bright-red dots on the rust-colored stain.

She expected to be ill, horrified. But a strange inner calm swept Deedra. She had the sense that this blood-letting was preordained, guided by some unseen hand, as symbolic as friends slicing fingertips and pressing the cuts together in a bonding that lasted forever. A rite. A passage. Something she needed in order to move on and let go. She felt Freddie nearby and knew she'd been brought to this very spot to say a final farewell to the person who'd been father, confessor and friend.

Instead of grief consuming her, overwhelming her, strength of spirit and soul stole into her. She smiled through a blur of warm tears and murmured, "Good-bye, my friend. And thank you."

"Dee? Dee? Are you shot?" Beau cried.

The fear in his voice chased the numbness from her, brought the pain of her torn flesh sharp, stinging. "No. Oh, God, Beau, are you hurt?"

"No," he said it in a way that reinforced what they both knew: the sniper meant for her to die, not him.

Beau shifted to a crouch, one hand pressing her down, the other withdrawing his gun from its holster. "Stay here. And keep low."

"No, Beau, don't!" She grabbed his sleeve. As certain as she'd been a moment ago, now she feared she could be wrong. What if the sniper wasn't someone who wanted her out of the way for a clear path to Beau? What if it was someone willing to take him out to get to her? She'd lost Callie and Freddie. She couldn't lose Beau, too. "Please, don't go after the sniper."

Sirens sounded in the distance. None of the bar patrons had come outside to see whether or not they were dead or dying, but someone had called 911. Beau hesitated, torn between looking for the sniper and staying with her. For once she wished he'd forget he was a cop and be a husband. For once she wished he'd choose her first.

The choice was taken from him as three police cars arrived on the scene followed by an ambulance.

A PARAMEDIC APPLIED SALVE and bandages, easing the sting in Deedra's palms, the ache in her knees. The provided painkiller even helped the throb in her lower back. But nothing relieved the niggling suspicion that

Freddie had died because he'd helped her get away from a killer, then betrayed her whereabouts.

She and Beau were escorted away from the crime scene and back downtown to the Butte police station. Throughout the hours of questioning that followed, a deep weariness settled over her. She thought the ordeal would never end. She'd lost complete track of time when Beau finally told her they could leave.

She stepped out into the night with the grace and energy of a zombie. The sun had gone, taking the warmth with it. A good thing, she decided. Cold penetrated her thin, ripped cotton clothes, robbed the lethargy attacking her limbs, cleared the cobwebs from her weary brain and restored her sense of caution, of observation.

Beau looked done in. He'd gone into The Copper Spittoon without his cane. Mr. Macho-Cop mode. Been without it all these hours, and he walked unsteadily now, the long day and his injury taking its toll.

"Are you hungry?" he asked, settling with a grimace on the driver's seat. He kept his voice light, but she caught a hint of fatigue, an edge of tension. "How does a twelve-ounce steak with all the trimmings sound?"

Food sounded wonderful. But a crowded restaurant? No. Deedra had been shot at, stared at and questioned until she felt as if she were the one suspected of wielding the rifle this afternoon. Her hands and knees were bandaged, her pants torn. She could not bear more strangers' questioning stares. Better something quick and anonymous. "I'd be happy with a cheeseburger and fries."

"And a double-caramel milkshake?"

She smiled, her mouth watering at the suggestion,

and the tightness in her chest broke loose for the first time on this awful day. When she'd been pregnant with Callie, she'd craved double-caramel shakes from Wally's Hamburger Shack. Beau never complained about running out for them. "I'm too hungry to wait until we get back to Buffalo Falls to eat."

"In that case, how about here?" He veered into a drive-through fast-food franchise and ordered. On a normal day, the fare couldn't hold a candle to Wally's, but tonight it tasted and smelled like Nirvana.

They ate as he drove, a sense of déjà vu settling over Deedra, a level of comfort she hadn't felt with Beau in a long time. She knew it couldn't last, but for the moment she enjoyed the feeling of just being with him. Of eating without talking. She couldn't tackle another serious subject. Not tonight. He seemed to feel the same.

She suspected he didn't want her to worry, but she caught his covert glances toward the rearview mirror. Knew from the set of his shoulders that he was alert to the possibility of the sniper following them. Finally she asked, "Anyone there we need to be concerned about?"

"No."

"Good."

They arrived without incident at the S bar S, rolling like sneak thieves under the high arch and along the half-mile lane. Vapor lamps topped peeler poles beside each of the outbuildings, casting a full-moon brightness over the yard. The buildings—house, garage, barn, stables and sheds—sported red paint with white trim. The house was an old-fashioned farmer's delight with a porch running clear around it, a lofted attic, a full basement and dormer windows at all the second-story bedrooms.

Glad that Pilar and Uncle Sean hadn't waited up to greet her, Deedra stared at the darkened house.

It had been home to four generations of Shanahans. Home to her. The only home in which she'd been happy. Could she be happy here again? Or was it too late? Had Beau found someone else? Were the rifts between them too many and too deep to repair? Had she come home not only to say goodbye to Callie but to Beau?

Her heart kicked a notch faster at the thought, and she felt a sudden uncertainty about being here. Every fear inside her screamed, "Run as fast and as far as you can." The thought brought her up cold. What had she been doing *but* running away? Prolonging the inevitable? Running away had cost her Freddie. Prolonging the inevitable might have cost her Beau. She had to stay and figure out what she wanted and where she wanted to be.

She had to find the person who'd taken Callie's life and stop him or her from killing again.

A flash of movement darting from the shadows sent the thought fleeing. Deedra jerked back, then almost laughed with relief. Three barn dogs. A long bark rent the quiet, but recognizing Beau's vehicle, the dogs quieted. Tails wagged.

"At least," Beau said wryly, "we'll have plenty of warning if any strangers decide to pay us a visit in the night."

She nodded, liking the feeling of security that that knowledge offered. The dogs gave up waiting for them to get out of the car and headed back toward the shadows. Watching them go, she noticed several vehicles parked beside the detached garage, including her rental.

"You need anything from your car?" Beau asked as he reached for his door handle.

"No." She hesitated as an unpleasant thought occurred. "Well, not unless you've given my things away."

"Nothing's changed here since you—"

He broke off, his face clouding. The tightness returned to her chest. She'd only been gone two months, but time didn't stand still. Everything changed. She and Beau were perfect examples. Once they'd been so much in love they couldn't keep their hands off each other. Now their touches held tension, discomfort.

She stepped out of the car, regret weighing heavily on her heart. The moon was full, the sky star-filled, the air crisper than in Butte. Fresher. She wondered if it heralded the beginning of fresh starts.

Beau leaned on his cane as they crossed the lighted brick walkway and porch. The door wasn't locked. No one locked their doors in Buffalo Falls. Not even Sheriff Beau Shanahan. Tonight he made an exception. The bolt slid home with a stiff clank. "I'm not risking an unwanted visitor somehow getting past our canine friends."

Deedra drew a shuddery breath, and her senses embraced the fragrance of lemon oil tinged with Mexican spices that were the staple of Pilar's culinary output.

Moonlight spilled through the obscured glass on either side of the door. The soft glow of illumination filled the foyer and showed the long hallway into the kitchen on her right, the dark living room on her left and the wide staircase ahead.

The house had a sturdy feel, as though it would withstand another four generations of Shanahans. The floors were solid hardwood covered with rich throw rugs, the theme as male as the hunting cabin. None of the women who'd married into this family had left as lasting an imprint as their husbands.

Not even Deedra.

Beau hooked his cane on the hall tree that had been built by his great-grandfather. He smoothed his hands over his hair, looking suddenly shy, self-conscious and vulnerable. He rubbed his hands down his thighs. Her gaze followed those big, powerful hands whose movements were slow and easy, and memories filled her mind, quickened her heart. Why did she have to recall those hands on *her,* soothing her, arousing her, satisfying her?

A flush of heat raced across her skin.

"Could you help me off with my boots? It's not so easy with this leg, you know? And Pilar will have my hide if I leave heel marks on her floors."

"Will she ever." Deedra laughed softly. "Sit."

She motioned to the hall tree seat. He sat, and she knelt before him. Mindful of her bandaged palms, she gently grasped the boot on his sore leg. She tugged. The boot resisted. She tugged harder.

"That's not the way you used to take off my boots."

She blushed, her gaze colliding with his. Heat seemed to leap between them, some sort of charged energy. To get away from it more than anything else, she stood and turned her back to him. Bent at the waist, she took his boot between her thighs. His leg brushed hers, the pressure intimate. She struggled to ignore her body's reaction, but Beau's big hands grabbed her hips. The touch jarred her, sent jolts of desire coursing through her.

She pulled the boot away from him as he pulled her hips toward him. The boot seemed determined to stay on. She yanked with all her might; Beau yanked her back at the same time. The suction gave. The boot slipped off and Deedra landed on his lap. He was rock hard beneath her. As turned on as she. *Yeah, this was how they used to do it. Exactly how.*

She scrambled to her feet. "I...I didn't h-hurt you, did I?"

He just looked at her, his glance a smoldering, exploring caress. "Are you still cold?"

His voice came out husky, making her aware of her tingling nipples, hard and visible beneath her blouse. As visible as his own arousal.

"No. I...no." She spun away, embarrassed at the physical evidence of the passion his very nearness stirred. One thing had not changed, not since that first day they'd met. Whatever it was—an unnameable electricity, a feral attraction—lived on, ignited by any connecting gaze between them.

He cleared his throat and lifted his other foot. "Please."

She hesitated, then drew a shaky breath, knowing the danger of touching him, wanting to touch him, wanting him to touch her. Her breath shuddered out. Her senses seemed heightened. Her nerve endings sensitive beyond anything near normal. Her skinned shins and palms tingled as she gingerly gathered the second boot by the heel and pulled away from him. The boot inched toward her. She tugged harder. Her shoes slipped on the polished floor. She felt her balance give and clamped tighter on to the boot. Jerked harder. The boot stayed snug.

She gave one final yank. As unexpectedly as the

other, this boot zipped off. Beau caught her wrists, keeping her on her feet. The warmth of his flesh touching hers spiraled heat from his hold straight into her heart, into her bloodstream, warming the part of her that had been cold for the past six months.

Moonlight stroked his blue-black hair, setting it and his eyes ablaze. Her throat tightened, and her gaze snagged on his mouth. That delicious, dangerous mouth. Here was the Beau she'd fallen in love with, the Beau she'd wanted to have babies with, to raise a family with.

The Beau she wanted still.

He pulled her to him, and she went without hesitation, slipping onto his lap, straddling him. Deedra's gaze locked with Beau's. His incredible emerald eyes burned into her, a pure green fire that carried her out of herself and into a realm vibrating with a shimmering, intimate beat.

The provocative melody filled her head, sang against her ears, along her nerves, through her veins. Her breath went soft. The bands of tightness in her chest snapped, and she felt freed of all restraint, freed to imbibe in the pleasures of the body, a she-warrior reunited with her *beau sabreur*.

Beau even looked the part, his ebony hair mussed, his chin hours too long from its last shave, his expression carnal. She caught his jaw in both hands. Whiskers bit the tender flesh of her fingertips, and the tiny pricks caused echoing twinges in her depths.

She brushed her lips against his.

He sucked in a sharp breath and emitted a tantalized groan. "Ah, Dee."

Beau didn't move though, didn't touch her, just held her with that gaze, with the lure of his thighs between hers. Need shivered through her. But she would not hurry. She traced her finger over his full bottom lip, across the arched upper one. His tongue flicked against her fingertip, wet, hot, enticing.

She sighed, leaned into him and gently licked that eager mouth with slow, slick swipes until his lips parted and she was tasting him, remembering, reliving, reawakening.

He smelled deliciously of Old Spice and onions, but he tasted sweeter than anything to touch her palate in months. Her senses gave a joyous leap as the kiss deepened and deepened. At length she pulled back, her breath rapid, fierce. Passion boiled in her core.

Impatience nipped at her. She burrowed her fingers between the snaps of his shirt, aching to touch him, all of him. The shirt quickly fell away, baring his broad shoulders, his muscled arms, the silken ebony hair on his powerful chest. She gasped as if seeing him for the first time. He was a man sculpted of God's best material, balance and bone, sinew and heart, all male.

And at this moment he belonged only to her.

Her hands feasted on his warm flesh, felt the sensuous tattoo of his heart.

He peeled off her blouse, her bra, as eager to touch her as she was to be touched. Her nipples beaded against the gentle abrasion of his work-roughened palms and tingling thrills spiraled through her when he took possession of first one breast and then the other. She arched against his hungry mouth, throwing her head back in ecstasy, crying his name.

He swept her to him, kissing her, quieting her noisy sighs of pleasure, and she realized they could be caught. They were not alone in the house. The thought heightened her arousal, her urgency. She clawed at his belt buckle, struggled free from her own pants. They were soon skin to skin, as naked as they'd been coming into this world, as exposed as one person could be to another. An intimacy of both body and soul.

For the first time in six months, Deedra felt happiness burning up from her very depths. She rubbed against Beau, laughing softly at the joy of caressing him, each sensation new yet familiar, teasing, tempting. He gave a growl of pleasure. "Enough, woman. You're making me crazed."

With that, he lifted her, bringing her down on him, filling her, stretching her, drawing erotic moans from her. His heat felt so hot she thought she'd burn to ashes, but the fire was liquid, melting, intoxicating. They rocked together in the feral dance of lovers, and the shimmering pulse-beat vibrated faster and faster.

Ecstasy ruled this magical, mystical realm, a physical, spiritual celebration lifting her toward the heavens and into a shattering star burst of erotica. Crystal white sparks of delight exploded within her, shooting from her core to every other part of her.

"Oh, Beau," she cried and fell against him, kissing his neck, clinging to him as he clung to her.

And finally, finally Deedra felt as if she'd come home.

"Beau?" Uncle Sean's gruff voice came from the second floor. "That you, boy?"

Deedra and Beau tensed. She wanted off his lap, wanted her clothes. He held her tight. "Go back to bed, Sean. I'm just locking up."

"You okay?" The upper hall creaked. Sean was walking toward the stairs. "Sounded like you might have fallen and needed some help."

"No. I'm fine." Beau assured him. He released

Deedra, and she scrambled for her clothes. Beau grabbed his pants off the floor. "Sorry I woke you."

Deedra darted into the living room, tugging on her panties.

Sean called out. "All right...if you're sure."

"I'm positive."

Deedra fumbled with her bra. Upstairs, the hallway creaked again as Sean retreated. The door to his room bumped shut, and she blew out a taut breath.

"Oh, my God. I feel like a naughty teenager," she whispered. "Didn't someone tell him I was with you?"

"I'm sure the ranch hands talked of nothing else once they returned from the cabin." Beau kept his voice low, too. "In fact, expecting you're with me is likely all that kept Sean from coming down those stairs."

He sat there, buck naked, one leg in his undershorts, grinning at her. He thought this was funny. She felt her mouth begin to curve upward. A laugh slipped from her, then another and another. Beau laughed, too. It was the first time they'd shared such a moment since... since they'd delighted in some antic or other of Callie's.

A floorboard creaked upstairs. Deedra froze. Beau sobered. Her eyes grew round, and she crammed her legs into her slacks.

"We'd better get to bed before Sean comes down again." Beau tugged on his underwear and grabbed his cane. "I'll be right back as soon as I've locked the rest of the house."

She watched him limp to the kitchen as she fumbled into her blouse. Weariness seeped back into her limbs. It had been one hell of a day—death stalking them at every turn. But milestones had been made, too. She and

Beau had finally broken through the wall that had separated them for so long. Finally made the first steps toward each other. She wasn't fooling herself into thinking they were all the way back, but it was a start in the right direction.

As long as he stayed on her side, they might even make it.

"Ready?" Beau gathered his shirt and jeans from the floor.

She took them from him. "Come on, cowboy. Let's hit the hay."

She spun toward the stairs, and Beau kissed the nape of her neck. She smiled and nuzzled him, then pulled away and started upstairs, looking forward to spending the night spooned against him. The hallway split at the upper landing, she and Beau occupied the west wing, Uncle Sean the east.

The Shanahan men had all been tall, and the four-poster king-size bed that stood in the center of the master suite was as old as the house, built to accommodate Beau's great-grandfather, the tallest of the clan at six-nine. The armoire and dresser belonged to the same era as the bed. Beau's mother had chosen to offset all the dark wood with mint-green fabrics and beige accents. Deedra had left it as she'd found it.

She placed Beau's clothes on the chair by the dresser and turned down the bedspread while he used the bathroom. He emerged within minutes, took one look at the bed and sighed.

"Ah, that looks like heaven." He'd shaved and showered, his hair damp. He kissed her neck again, then yawning, sank to the mattress. "Hurry."

"I'll be right there."

The bathroom was tile and glass, nearly as large as

the bedroom with a huge walk-in closet. She'd thought she'd never see it again and had never imagined she'd feel this glad to be standing here, staring at her pale face in that wide expanse of mirror over the double sinks.

Pain grazed her lower belly, and she realized, as good as making love with Beau had felt, it might not have been in her best interest physically. Her medication was in a bag in the rental car. She hated to send Beau out for it, but knew she'd need it before morning.

She took a quick shower and dressed in a favorite nightgown, one Beau had bought her on their honeymoon. He liked the way it hugged her curves. But it didn't hug her now, she realized, glancing at her reflection. The gown now hung on her like a gunny sack—her curves all sharp angles, nothing soft or feminine. She knew she'd lost weight, but not this much.

Beau hadn't said a thing. But he must have noticed. Feeling self-conscious, she came out of the bedroom. "Beau, I need you to do me a huge fav—"

His noisy snore interrupted her.

A cramp swept her belly again. She had to get her medicine. She glanced at the bedroom door but made no move toward it. With Beau asleep, she felt suddenly alone again. Fearful. What if the sniper was outside lying in wait? Hoping to catch her doing something as stupid as sneaking out to her car in the middle of the night? She shook her head. *Damn it, Deedra. Get a grip.* If the sniper was out there the dogs would have sounded an alert.

No dogs barked. She could dart to her car, grab her bag and duck back into the house without anyone the wiser. Except for the dogs. If they recognized her scent, they might not bark, but they would jump all over her with their dirty paws and slobbering tongues. She didn't have the strength to deal with that right now. She returned to the bathroom for aspirin and snuggled into the bed beside Beau. She fell asleep within seconds.

She awoke to find herself alone. This wasn't the first time she'd awakened without Beau in this big bed, but for the first time in a long lot of mornings, it didn't depress her. She climbed out from under the sheets and stretched. A cramp crossed her stomach. She would have to see the doctor soon. But this morning, she had to face Pilar and Uncle Sean.

She straightened the bed, then hurried into the bathroom and froze. Scrawled across the mirror in blood-red lettering were the words:

If I can get to you here,
I can get you anywhere, bitch.

Chapter Eight

Deedra's scream cut through Beau like a knife. He dropped his mug on the tiled kitchen counter. Ceramic shards and coffee flew in every direction. "Dee!"

"*Dios!*" Pilar cried, her hand moving to her ample bosom. "I thought you say she all better."

"She is." Beau ran as if he'd never injured his leg, moving up the stairs as though he'd healed overnight.

Pilar followed, mumbling so rapidly in Spanish the only word he caught was "*loco.*"

As he tore up the stairs, he prayed Pilar was wrong, prayed the Dee he'd been with yesterday had come home to stay. But his heart stopped at the sight of her curled on the bathroom floor, hugging her knees to her chest.

"Sweetheart, what happened?" He squatted beside her and folded her against him. Her body trembled in his embrace. "What's the matter?"

"Oh, Señor Beau!" Pilar gasped and pointed to the mirror. "Look what she done!"

Beau's gaze jerked to the mirror; his throat thickened with dread. The words were written in lipstick, the same shade of red as the tube Dee kept in the top drawer beside the sink. "Sweetheart, wh-what—"

Her wide gray eyes lifted to meet his. Hurt and disbelief shone out at him.

"You think *I* wrote this?" Her voice inched higher. "You *both* think *I* wrote this?"

Fury steamed off Deedra, sending a chill through Beau. She'd made it clear before she'd run away that his lack of support had eroded their relationship. That he could even consider *she* would have written this threat underscored everything she'd been telling him. His heart sank. In that single moment of doubt, he'd erased the intimacy, the closeness they'd experienced the previous night.

But what did she expect? Had she forgotten that she'd been less than rational these last six months? That she'd taken off without telling anyone where she was going, leaving them to fear she'd been snatched by some serial killer, tortured and murdered, or that she might be wandering the country without knowing where or who she was. "Are you saying someone got in here while you were sleeping?"

"It wasn't me," she ground out between clenched teeth.

Pilar, Beau noticed, was gaping at Dee as though she didn't recognize her. He supposed the short blond hair and the noticeable weight loss had thrown the housekeeper. Pilar stepped back toward the doorframe. "Señor Beau and I was in the kitchen. No one comes in. We would hear."

"I didn't do this." Deedra touched her short blond hair self-consciously and turned accusing eyes to Beau. "Did you unlock the front door this morning?"

"Of course." He struggled to keep his tone even. "That door is always unlocked during the day."

"You locked the house last night?" Pilar's black

eyes flashed with surprise. She crossed herself. "*Dios.
What this world it comes to when neighbor no trust
neighbor?*"

Deedra's face was eerily pale, except for the
splotches of red on both cheeks. She pushed to her feet,
seeming to gather some inner strength, and clutched
her robe to her chest, holding her trembling chin high.
"Beau, could you bring my bag in from my rental car.
I have some pills I need to take."

"Pilar, we'll be down for breakfast in a few
minutes," he said, dismissing the housekeeper. She left
as though happy to escape. Deedra stepped into the
walk-in closet without glancing at him, and Beau
wanted to kick himself. This was not the homecoming
he'd planned for her after last night.

Damn it all. Yesterday had frayed their respective
mettles to the snapping point, but somehow they'd
managed to hang on and come out the other side ahead
of where they'd been these past few months. At least,
that's how he'd felt this morning when he'd awakened
to find her beautiful face on the pillow beside his.

He realized now that he'd deluded himself. She was
still as fragile, maybe more so, than when she'd last
been home. Her weight loss should have told him she
was running on raw nerves. More frazzled than before.
He thought of the pills and wondered whether they
were some kind of mood regulators.

She intruded on his thoughts. "I'll get dressed and
meet you downstairs."

"I'm not going yet." He reached above her head for
the camera on the closet shelf. "I want to photograph
that writing. For evidence."

She gave him a leery glance, judging his motives,
he suspected. She didn't quite trust him. He wasn't sure

how to regain her trust, either. In fact, if he were honest with himself, he wasn't sure he fully trusted her. Maybe there had been too much damage to their relationship for them to recover.

He cleared his throat. "After breakfast I'll speak with the ranch hands and Uncle Sean. Maybe one of them noticed somebody coming into the house this morning."

He saw her shoulders shift as if something weighty had been lifted from them. "Thank you. Beau, before you start taking pictures, could you get my bag?"

"Sure." He set the camera on the bathroom counter and hurried out to her car. When he returned, Dee was dressed in jeans and a T-shirt. Both were baggy.

She frowned at her image in the full-length mirror. "My clothes are too big."

He bit back the urge to comment, figuring this was one of those times when no matter what a guy said, it would be the wrong response. He gave her the overnight case, and then went back to the camera.

Through the lens, he studied the lipstick graffiti. The letters had been formed with hard, sharp strokes as if written in searing anger. He focused on the wording, and the hair on his nape prickled. He'd seen this printing. Recently. But where? It wasn't Dee's, but another woman's. Damn it. Who? The answer flickered on the edges of his memory.

The rattle of pills against plastic sent the memory fleeing. Deedra had dug a medicine bottle from the overnight bag he'd brought her. She peered into the depths of the plastic container, then said, "I'll need to see Dr. Haynes and get these refilled. Set up my surgery, too."

"I'll take you in later this morning if you can get an appointment."

"Good." She tugged the top off the pill container.

"Dee." He pointed to the message on the mirror. "Does this writing look familiar to you?"

She bristled, the pill bottle tilted over her upturned palm. "I told you I didn't do it."

"Dee, if we're going to figure out who's trying to kill you, we have to work together. Because, so far, working separately hasn't done us any good."

"That's for damned sure." Two pills landed in her palm.

"Then can we call a truce?"

She blew out a taut breath and nodded. "Okay."

He pointed to the mirror. "Does this handwriting look familiar to you?"

She stared at the writing, tugging a disposable cup from its dispenser and filling it with water. "You know, there *is* something... Those, uh, curlicued *E*s. I've seen them recently somewhere..." She raised the pills to her mouth, then stopped, her eyes rounding as an answer dawned on her. "Oh, my God, Beau. The woman who writes you love notes."

He swore and slapped a hand against his thigh. *That was it.* "You're right. It's her."

Deedra's fist curled around the pills, and she stepped closer to him, her gaze blazing with accusation. "Who is she?"

"Dee, I swear to you on...on Callie's grave, I have no idea." He touched his chest over his heart with both hands. "The relationship she describes between us in those mash notes is a delusion. Not only have I never been with this woman, I don't even know her."

He wanted to touch her, to pull her into his arms

and assure her of his sincerity with every ounce of his being. But she held herself too stiff, resistance tight in her expression. He dropped his hands to his sides. She'd have to decide. Either she trusted him, or...

She lifted her hand to her mouth to take the pills and Beau felt a shock of fear. *Oh, Lord, what if...?* He grabbed her hand. She yelped in startled pain and dropped the pills. "What are you doing?"

"The pills. Your car wasn't locked. She could have—"

He didn't need to finish the sentence. Deedra stepped back as though he'd slapped her. Her gaze fell to the dropped pills. She bent and gathered the two capsules, and then offered them to Beau. He collected the nearly empty bottle and replaced them.

"I believe you." She spoke so softly it took him a moment to realize what she'd said.

The band unwound from his chest, easing his breathing. "I'll call Nora Lee, get her out here to dust for fingerprints."

She frowned. "Is it likely she'll find any? Even crime-committing morons know to wear gloves these days."

"Then I'll call Heck, hire a private forensics lab from Butte. They'll go over this room and the bedroom with a fine-tooth comb, as well as analyze these capsules."

She frowned. "Haven't we compromised the scene already? Added our DNA to whatever might have been left behind?"

"Yeah, but these days more crimes are solved with science than old-fashioned puzzle work. The team can eliminate us and Pilar, and with any luck, they'll find a hair or fiber or other evidence to point us in the right direction. Maybe on one of the pills, if not the container. Maybe near the bed, or on the counter, the mirror, the cabinet.''

"The lipstick.'' Deedra swept open the drawer where she kept the tube of lip gloss that matched the lettering on the mirror and dug through the array of cosmetics. "It's not here.''

Beau grabbed the waste basket. "Not here, either.''

"She took it with her.''

"That doesn't mean she wasn't careless.'' But the look Dee gave him echoed his own doubts on *that* subject. So far they had nothing on this woman except her delusional mash notes, and since he'd never even guessed she was at the heart of the attacks on Dee, he'd tossed most of those—or handled them without thought. But this time the woman had gotten careless. Coming into their home, into their bedroom, she'd increased the chances that she'd left behind a clue or two to her identity.

For the first time in a long time, he felt encouraged.

His stomach gave a hungry growl. "Come on, let's go see what Pilar fixed for breakfast.''

NORA LEE ANDERSON ARRIVED around lunchtime with a man and woman from the Butte forensics lab Beau had contacted. Deedra had met Nora Lee when Clyde DeMarco was still sheriff, a couple of months after Callie went missing. She wore a uniform that had enough police regulation gear attached to dwarf her compact figure, and an air that warned she could more than handle her job. She had the high cheekbones and coloring of an ice queen from the fjords of Norway, slanted frost-blue eyes and a full, serious mouth. Her hair was short, a snowy cap. For all her chilly exterior,

Deedra had found her sympathetic and warm during some of her hardest hours. She would never forget that kindness.

They exchanged greetings, and Beau led the three to the bedroom. Deedra retreated to the kitchen.

Sean Shanahan was seated at the breakfast table in the bay window that overlooked the barn and corrals.

Over the rim of his coffee cup, he locked Deedra with a cold stare.

Her heart clutched, and she wished she'd accompanied Beau upstairs with Nora Lee and the forensics team. She tore her gaze from his and circled the counter to the half-full coffeepot. Sean's gaze drilled into her, assessing, judging. She'd always gotten the impression that he hadn't approved of her, hadn't thought she was good enough for Beau. Holding the pot, she glanced at him. "More coffee?"

"No, thanks." He shoved away from the table. He stood almost as tall as her husband, but there had always been something more imposing about this man. The hardships he'd suffered early in his life had turned his dense ebony hair completely silver by the time he reached thirty. Now, at forty-seven, he wore it in a crew cut. His green eyes were shades paler than Beau's, but just as mesmerizing, as intense.

She felt pinned by them now.

He placed his empty mug in the sink. "For Beau's sake, I'm glad you've turned up alive and relatively well. But you ought to be tarred and feathered for what you put him and the rest of us through—thinkin' God-knows-what might've befallen you. Scourin' the country for you. Havin' to accept that you might not be alive. How'd you expect Beau to take that comin' on the heels of losin' his sweet baby girl?"

"I...I..." Heat flooded her cheeks. Beau hadn't told her they'd scoured the country for her. But of course he would have. He'd probably rousted Freddie about her whereabouts, too. But obviously her old friend hadn't seen fit to set his mind at ease. Damn it all. "I'm sorry for causing such distress."

"You oughta be." Sean was no stranger to distress. Or loss. His first wife died weeks after their wedding, of an aneurysm. He met and married Jenny five years later. That marriage lasted a whole year and a half. According to Sean, Jenny had a worse malady than his first wife: wanderlust.

She'd hated ranch life. Had wanted him to give it up. As if it weren't in his blood. His soul. She'd run off with one of his ranch hands. He'd never gotten over these two blows to his heart. His ego. Some females, he now claimed, as though it were God's own truth, were not meant to be Shanahan women. He could see it in their eyes.

Every time she heard him say this, she knew he meant *her* eyes.

"I was desperate, Sean," she explained, not expecting him to understand, but needing to be heard. "I didn't have time to think about anything or anyone else. Just escape. Or die."

His glare hardened. "Most people in those shoes would've turned to family for help."

She bit down her growing anger. Furious with herself that his words could sting so deeply. How easy it was for him. How black-and-white. He had something she'd never had. Roots. Family ties that bound his very soul. He didn't do anything without considering how his actions might affect the unit as a whole.

He could never comprehend the desperation she'd

grown up with, could never know what it was to live in her world where preservation hinged on self.

It struck her now that she had never let go of that belief. Never allowed herself to feel totally a part of this family. She hadn't known how. Still didn't. Could such a thing be learned? Could someone who'd disconnected before she'd reached her teens ever plug in again? "All I can do is apologize, Sean, but not for running. Left with the same choices, I'd do it again."

"Let's see that you don't have reason to do it again." But the look in his eyes said he expected her to do exactly that at the first opportunity.

She wanted nothing more than to disabuse him of the notion. "I'm not planning on going anywhere. I'm here to stand and fight."

"It's about time you started acting like a Shanahan."

So, that was what this was all about: she'd embarrassed him. Smudged the Shanahan name. She would be the hot topic at Granny Jo's diner for weeks to come. She suspected if Sean had his way, she wouldn't be a Shanahan. Well, he might just get that wish. And soon. Beau being so quick to believe she might have written that vile message on the bathroom mirror had shown her that she was jumping the gun thinking they could bridge the gap between them by making love. Physical passion burned bright but not necessarily long. Great sex was not binding. It did not glue marriages together over the long haul.

But she had more important things to worry about first: like who could slip onto the ranch and into the house without anyone paying them the least attention?

Chapter Nine

"Why didn't she just kill me this morning, Beau?"
Deedra had been able to think of nothing but the
killer's threat since leaving the house and heading out
into open territory. Beau was driving her to her doctor's appointment. Buffalo Falls loomed on the horizon.
. He scanned the road ahead and behind. Distracted,
too. "What do you mean?"

"Why write a threat on the bathroom mirror? Why
did she want me to know she could get to me? What's
the point of playing games at this juncture?"

Beau grew thoughtful, then sighed. "Damned if I
can figure it."

"After her blatant attacks yesterday, it really doesn't
make sense, does it?"

"Hell, I don't know." His jet-black eyebrows
scrunched together beneath the brim of his Stetson.
"Maybe it's too much to ask that it make sense. I
mean, considering she's nuttier than Pilar's black-
walnut cookies."

Deedra's palms dampened and her scalp prickled.
Street life had taught her that it was best to deal head-
on with most things that came at her. Except the crazies. She shivered, recalling. One night, another run-

away she'd befriended attempted to help a bag lady. The bag lady had thought the girl intended to steal something from the precious store of treasures she toted around in a grocery cart. She flashed a switchblade and plunged it into the runaway's belly faster than Deedra could yell, "Look out!"

She could still smell the dying girl's blood. She shed the awful memory but couldn't shirk the message in that lesson. If the woman who wanted her dead actually was insane, heaven help her. "How can we keep ahead of someone who doesn't *think* like a normal person?"

His sexy mouth firmed. "We have to think like a crazy person."

"How do we do that?"

"I'm not sure yet."

"Great." She shivered, wanting to scream, wanting to shred something with her bare hands.

"I'm sorry, Dee. I didn't mean to make you feel worse. We'll figure something out. Don't be scared."

"How do I manage that after yesterday? I'm afraid to show my face on the street for fear of getting shot."

"She won't pull anything in town." He stroked her wrist, his fingers warm, tender. His touch felt good. Too good. Reassuring her that she wasn't alone. She ached to embrace the feeling but she couldn't. She didn't trust it. Didn't trust herself. Didn't trust that Beau wouldn't abandon her again when she most needed him.

She pulled away, out of his reach. "If she's as unhinged as we suspect, Beau, she'll try anything anywhere."

"I don't think she's that kind of unhinged."

She pushed her hands through her short hair, wishing he'd stop staring at her mouth as though he wanted to devour it, wishing she didn't share that feeling. "You mean, 'crazy like a fox'?"

"Yeah. Think about it, Dee. She needs to function normally somewhere. I'd wager my brand-new silver-studded saddle that Buffalo Falls is her home turf. If it weren't, she couldn't move around without standing out like an Angus in a field of longhorns."

They passed Wally's Hamburger Shack, and Deedra glanced askance at it, not thinking of double-caramel milkshakes today, but of this disarming town. On the surface, it seemed innocent, but she knew now that she'd judged this book by its pastoral cover. She hadn't even suspected the same kind of twisted nastiness that existed everywhere else in the world thrived just beneath the clapboard storefronts in this most benign of places.

Beau drove onto Cody Street. The facade of Dr. Haynes's offices resembled an Old-West saloon, right down to the double swinging doors. The single-story building took up the entire block. An attorney rented the office directly across the street. Few cars and fewer pedestrians moved about this afternoon, but she and Beau might have been a common sight for all the attention they drew.

The doctor's waiting room was another story. Deedra braced herself for a slew of curious glances and bold questions, but she might have been invisible. The six women patients seated in the doctor's stiff plastic chairs, along with the nurse and the receptionist, had eyes only for Beau.

He tipped his hat, and his mouth lifted at one corner, the beginning of a self-conscious grin. The women sighed in concert. Deedra shook her head. He could charm the mane from a Palomino if he set his mind to it. She suspected now he was using that charm to take the spotlight from her, and she had to admit, she owed him one for doing so.

"Ladies." He leaned on his cane like a man who'd fall down without it, like a man who might need some assistance from any one or all of these ladies.

"Afternoon, Sheriff," several voices sang together.

"We hear you had some excitement out at your hunting lodge yesterday." Zora Cross pushed her eyeglasses up the bridge of her ninety-year-old nose, as though the closer the lens, the better the view.

"A real shoot-out." McKenna Broom, all of thirteen and starry-eyed with infatuation, sighed.

The others joined the discussion, asking questions, offering opinions.

No one mentioned the return of his missing wife, she noted. A fact Deedra found odd considering the smoothly oiled gossip machine operating in this town. She gazed from woman to woman. No doubt about it, Beau was a regular babe magnet. She swallowed over a knot of frustration. The sniper wanted Beau to herself. So, it seemed, did every woman in this room. Damn. If this small sampling was any indication, their suspect list would contain the entire female population of Buffalo Falls.

A bone-deep exhaustion swept her. The task of unmasking the stalker seemed suddenly more than daunting. Impossible. Too much to deal with, given her present physical and mental challenges. It would be so easy to just cry Uncle! And what? Let the she-devil win?

That she could even think of quitting, sobered Deedra. She fought down the defeatist musings, her gaze steadied on her handsome husband and his flock of admirers. A new, different thought sliced the fog of negativity, something so obvious it hadn't occurred to her earlier. The killer wouldn't be looking at Beau with longing, but eyeing her with daggers. But no one was paying *her* the least attention. No, edit that. One woman was looking at her and shaking her head in sympathy. Dr. Haynes's nurse, Cassidy Brewer.

Cassidy, a former rodeo queen, a champion barrel racer, wore her dark-golden hair down her back in a braid as thick as a child's arm. A perpetual tan showed off the highlights in her blond tresses and accentuated her wide indigo eyes. She had an earthiness, a natural sensuality that other women felt and men found irresistible. As far as Deedra knew, however, she'd never been married. Or had a serious romantic relationship.

Was it too much of a stretch to wonder if unrequited feelings for Beau kept her single?

Deedra strode to the counter where she stood. "I have a two-o'clock appointment."

"Must be annoying to have to beat off the competition." Cassidy nodded toward Beau, who was now surrounded by women.

Competition? The idea struck Deedra as ludicrous. Then again, "competition" was exactly what her deranged stalker considered her. She kept her voice low. "I'm Beau's wife. I don't need to compete for his attention."

Cassidy looked unconvinced. "Your lips to God's ears."

Deedra's temper flared, and she curled her fists at her sides, fighting the urge to slap the smirk from the nurse's mouth. For all she knew, Cassidy Brewer might be a dangerous killer. Deedra gazed at the other woman's ruddy hands and wondered whether she could shoot a gun as well as she could ride a horse. And did that even make sense? Wouldn't a nurse's weapons of choice more likely run to drugs or pills? Like *her* pills?

A shiver tracked her spine. A nurse would know how to get into a hospital. Know how to switch the stored blood of patients.

"Nora Lee just beeped me," Beau said, halting her train of thought. She wanted to tell him what had just occurred to her. That Cassidy Brewer was a definite suspect. But not here. Not now. Not with Cassidy's glare boring into her.

Beau shifted his weight on the cane and dipped close so that only she could hear him. "Apparently something needs my personal attention."

Her gaze slammed into his, her heart skipping with hope. "Has she heard from the forensics lab?"

"I don't know. I don't want to phone from here and ask."

"Then I'm coming with you."

"No. You need to see the doctor."

"No, I—" But he was right. She did need to see the doctor. She could not put it off. She relented. "Okay, I'll stay."

He studied her. "Will you be all right?"

She heard the ladies sigh at his concern for her and, mentally, she rolled her eyes. She'd been taking care of herself since her teens; she could survive an hour or so in a doctor's office. "Of course."

"Are you sure?"

"Yes. Go on."

"I'll be back by the time you're finished." He squeezed her lower arm reassuringly, and, despite her determination not to rely too much on Beau, she knew she did. "I'll be fine."

BY THE TIME she'd finished with Dr. Haynes, prescription in hand and a tentative surgical date set, Beau had not returned. Deedra considered sitting on one of the plastic chairs to wait and decided she'd rather have some air and get away from the overt glances the newly arrived patients sent her.

Without Beau running interference the townsfolk seemed like some noxious cloud billowing from a copper pit, sucking all the oxygen in its wake. She hurried outside. The air tasted so fresh she indulged in several lungs full as she scanned the street for Beau's car. What was keeping him? Had his deputy's call had something to do with the sniper after all?

Or was the sniper here somewhere, watching her through the sight of her rifle? Maybe she should go back inside. No. She wasn't going back into that waiting room for anything. She glanced around for a pay phone, but couldn't find one. Her gaze landed on the attorney's office. She'd call the station from there. She darted across the street, praying Beau was right about the sniper not risking shooting her in town.

Gold lettering etched the obscured glass door: T. R. Rudway, Attorney at Law. She reached for the knob. The door swung inward, and she stood face-to-face with a very pregnant woman around nineteen. Deedra stared at the other woman's distended stomach and her heart clenched, squeezing out envy and grief and a slew of other emotions that weakened her knees.

"Watch where you're going," the nineteen-year-old snapped.

Deedra caught her breath. She straightened and moved back, offering an awkward apology. The pregnant woman shouldered past her, mumbling under her breath something that Deedra couldn't quite hear but that most certainly maligned her parentage.

"Nice talk, *Mommy*," Deedra said.

"Screw you!"

Deedra resisted the impulse to continue this spitting match, to vent her frustrations on someone she didn't even know. She let the door shut the woman out, but Deedra's temper simmered, and she knew it wasn't just the teenager's attitude but the unfairness of it all that had her riled. What law of the universe made someone like that foul-mouthed youngster a mother and left *her* unable to bear another child?

Fighting off a spate of self-pity, she forced herself to focus on her surroundings. Rich cherry wood paneling graced the walls and extended to the furnishings. The dark hues were offset by accessories in varying tones of beige and gold and a couple of huge potted palms.

There was something cooling, calming about the space, as though a soft breeze swept through it. None of this went with her mental image of an attorney named T. R. Rudway. She'd pictured a two-bit ambulance chaser.

This office, however, bespoke success and big money. It belonged in a cosmopolitan city. Not Buffalo Falls. So why was it here? Surely this community couldn't dredge up enough annual legal business to justify the expense or the formality. In fact, she couldn't imagine any local farmer or rancher coming in here, their boots caked in cow or horse dung, to consult an attorney.

Just who were T. R. Rudway's clients? Was this lawyer doing something illegal right under Beau's nose? She wondered if he'd ever been here, ever even met

ol' T.R.—probably some potbellied good old boy dripping in gold and diamonds, bartering who knew what
kind of deals for wealthy lawbreakers.

There was no receptionist, but she heard voices in a
connecting room. The door to the inner office opened,
and a couple stepped through. Deedra knew designer
clothing, real gold and genuine diamonds, when she
saw them, but she didn't know this couple. Out-of-
towners, no doubt. Wealthy out-of-towners, just as
she'd figured.

The man spoke to someone in the office, his voice
dripping with a twang straight out of the Deep South,
"How soon before the adoption is final, Ms. Rudway?"

Ms. Rudway? T.R. was a woman?

A shapely brunette in a dove-gray suit filled the door
frame, clearing up all doubt of her gender. She wore
no jewelry. It would have been too much, given her
natural beauty. She was stunning. "Around three
weeks or so, Tom. The pregnancy is textbook normal.
As soon as the mother goes into labor, I'll notify you
and Lucille."

"We'll be able to take our baby straight home from
the hospital?" the woman asked, her accent as thick as
her husband's.

"Soon as the doctor releases him," the lawyer assured them.

Deedra shrank against the receptionist's desk, listening but not wanting to draw attention to herself. What
was a couple from some Southern state doing in a small
town in Montana arranging to adopt a baby? Why
weren't they making these arrangements in their home
state?

Or maybe Deedra was reading something sinister

into something innocent? Her mind flashed on the nineteen-year-old with attitude. Maybe she wasn't an unmarried, pregnant teen, but a surrogate mother. Maybe T. R. Rudway found women willing to bear babies for wealthy couples if the price was right. Or maybe she just specialized in private adoptions.

Deedra glanced around the outer office again. *Expensive* private adoptions. She and Beau had discussed adoption after learning she needed a hysterectomy. Actually, he'd suggested it; she'd dismissed it. She hadn't wanted any babies but their own. Now she felt a twinge of envy for the anticipation this couple must feel looking forward to that new infant.

"That'll be the best call of our lives." The man draped his arm around his wife and guided her toward the exit.

Deedra waited until the door shut to make her presence known. "Er, Ms. Rudway?"

T.R. jerked as if she'd been poked in the back. "Oh, I'm sorry, I didn't see you there. Are you my three-o'clock?"

"No. No." She stepped toward the attorney and saw a flicker of something in the woman's hazel eyes, something too dark and fleeting to identify. Perhaps caution. Deedra decided to test that wariness. "I was wondering if I might use your phone to call my husband...the sheriff."

Those same eyes rounded at the mention of Beau, and Deedra knew she'd struck a nerve of some kind. But she didn't expect the lawyer to say, "*You're* Deedra Shanahan?"

Deedra frowned. She didn't know this woman. But the attorney had obviously heard of *her*. "How did you...?"

T.R. laughed. "Besides the start of the Crazy Daze sales, which commence today, your return to town was the topic du jour this morning at Granny Jo's."

"No doubt." Deedra hated the heat charging up her cheeks. "Strangely, though, I can't say I've ever heard of you. So, I'm guessing you opened this office sometime in the past two months."

"Two months next week."

"From the look of things, business is good."

"Very." She pressed her card into Deedra's hand. "But a lawyer can always use new clients. If there's ever anything I can do for you...or Sheriff Shanahan...please don't hesitate to contact me."

To work out a contract? For adoption services? To sue someone? Whatever branch of the law T.R. practiced was not specified on the card resting in Deedra's palm. Deedra cleared her throat. "Sure, thanks. The phone?"

"Certainly." T.R. gestured to the one on the receptionist's desk, then strode to her office and shut the door.

Giving Deedra privacy?

Or was she listening in on an extension?

Deedra couldn't hear breathing on the phone line and almost laughed at her paranoia, even if she had good reason for it. She dialed the police station.

Heck Long answered. "Hello, Ms. Shanahan. No, I don't know where the sheriff is. Or anyone else. I just came in from patrol and found the office empty, but if you should see Beau before me, would you tell him that he's got some phone calls here? A couple of them are marked urgent. Huh, both from the same woman, a Missus or Miss Carter."

Deedra's heart skipped at the name, but in the next

second she cautioned herself against jumping to conclusions. Carter was a common enough surname. "Did
she leave a first name, a phone number?"

"Ah…yeah," he said, as though he were scanning
the message for details. "Yeah. They're both here.
First name's Nell. Nell Carter. Don't know what she'd
want with the sheriff, though. According to the phone
number she left, she was callin' from Butte."

It *was* Freddie's mother. What possible reason would
she have to call Beau? Perhaps Nell was trying to reach
her. No. She would have called the ranch, not the police station. Maybe she had. She promised Heck she
would pass along the messages, disconnected and dialed the ranch. Pilar answered, but said Deedra's call
was the first one all afternoon.

She hung up. A niggling unease gripped her. Nell
had called Beau. Not once. But twice. The messages
marked "urgent." Nell didn't even know Beau. She
would call Nell now if she hadn't cut up her long-
distance calling card two months ago.

Deedra made for the door, her mind turned inward
to the day Beau and she had visited Nell's house, the
day they'd found out Freddie had been murdered. Did
Nell know something about the murder she hadn't told
the police?

Deedra recalled seeing the curtain in the upstairs
window move—as if someone were there, hiding. At
the time she'd thought she might have imagined that
movement. Now she felt sure she hadn't. And the question was: Had Nell shut herself away from the outside
world in grief…or in fear?

She had to find Beau. Now. But he wasn't waiting
for her outside. The uneasiness gathered inside her like
a building storm. Where was he? What was keeping

him? The police station was only a few blocks away. She set out for it on foot, praying she'd run into him along the way.

Despite the warm afternoon, Deedra felt chilled, her skin prickly. Every step left her more jumpy. More anxious to reach Beau. But progress was impeded by the annual Crazy Daze summer sales T. R. Rudway had mentioned. Sidewalks were crowded with racks of clothes, bargain tables and shoppers.

She paid all of it little attention and was thankfully not accosted by any of the bargain hunters, but on Custer Street, a familiar face snagged her attention. The rude, pregnant teen she'd encountered earlier at the attorney's office. She was at the end of the street on the opposite side.

Curious, Deedra watched her turn into the last door on the block, into the office of Dr. Elle Warren. Deedra's psychologist. Deedra stopped midstep, a rush of unpleasant memories hitting her. She'd poured her heart out to Dr. Warren after Callie… Her throat tightened and began to ache as if someone were strangling her.

Dr. Warren's counseling had not helped her salvage her relationship with Beau, it had only increased her resentment of his neglect. But worse than that the sessions hadn't helped her accept and deal with the loss of her daughter…they had only increased her belief that Callie lived.

She'd had to run away from this town in order to face her daughter's death. She'd come home to lay her baby to rest. But once she'd driven back into this town, before she'd even reached the cemetery, the doubts had crept in again. And now, as she stood on this street, staring at Dr. Warren's office, she felt Callie's presence yet again.

Hope as gentle and strong as a baby's grip took hold of her heart, and though she tried to shake it off, to shove it away, she couldn't. God help her, she couldn't. Something snapped inside Deedra, split like the wall of a dam, a crack here, a crack there, held-back remembrances spilling out, trickling into her awareness. And then the cracks grew larger until the whole wall gave and memories gushed through her like a flash flood she couldn't outrun.

Moments of joy, moments of Callie, happy moments, loving moments. In the deluge of longing that claimed her senses, every other thought crashed away like uprooted trees, including her urgency to find Beau. All Deedra wanted was Callie.

She wandered into the nearest shop, the only three-level department store in town. Of their own volition, her feet carried her to the second floor, into the baby department. She roamed between the rows of infant wear, stopping and lifting a tin of baby powder from the shelf. She popped the seal and inhaled the talcum's sweet scent, recalling Callie damp and squirmy after her bath, laughing as Deedra dried her, powdered her, spread baby lotion over her delicate, silky skin.

The knot in her throat wound tighter. Tears stung her eyes. She fought them, absently clutching the tin to her aching heart, spinning away from the staring eye of the salesclerk. She had to get out of here. But as she moved to the exit, her gaze hooked on a slash of mint-green gingham poking from between a crush of sales items on a nearby rack. She stumbled forward and plucked the item free.

Her heart stopped. It was a puffy-sleeved, smock-topped dress with ribbons at the collar. Callie had worn a similar dress when she'd gone missing. Deedra dropped it and jerked back as if it were a live rattler that had just bitten her.

Tremors rocked her as if the earth were quaking, soon to crumble and suck her into a black hole. Only the laughter saved her. Pulled her back from the edge of the abyss.

A child's laugh.

Callie's laugh.

Deedra jerked around, wildly seeking her daughter. There! At the checkout counter. A woman she didn't recognize held a little girl with wavy black hair. Callie! She couldn't see the child's face, but she knew. *She knew.* Her heart that moments ago had stopped, now galloped. "Callie."

She kept her gaze locked on the raven hair and, like a pigeon on a course for home, started forward as if she had wings and could fly over all the obstacles between herself and her little girl. Of course, she couldn't. She rammed into a waist-high display. *No! No!* Diaper bags, stuffed toys and Deedra sprawled to the floor. The tin of talc she'd forgotten she still clutched, burst open spewing powder into an arc to rain down on the mess like some fragrant snowfall. Coughing and batting at her face and clothing, Deedra fought to untangle herself, fought the salesclerk trying to help her and bounded up.

The child and the woman had gone.

"No!" she groaned. Heartache and panic spread through her chest and into her head. She raced to the stairs. Then clambered down. Her frantic gaze scouted every aisle. Every exit. *There! Going out the door!* She tore through the store, ducking and weaving between the shoppers, nearly knocking over an elderly man, oblivious to the shocked and curious stares coming at her from every direction.

She hurried outside. Once again she searched the sidewalks. Her heart in her throat. Her breath a ragged pain in her chest. *There!* On the sidewalk ahead. She ran for the woman. "Stop! Give me back my child!"

The woman turned, took one look at Deedra, dropped her packages, swept up the little girl and ran, too. The child began to cry. The woman ran faster and ducked into a doorway ahead. Deedra arrived right behind her, panting. *Oh, God, she was finally going to have Callie back.*

It took her a moment to recognize her surroundings. The Buffalo Falls Police Station. The woman she'd been chasing looked about the age of Deedra's mother. She was round and soft and obviously terrified. She cowered near Heck Long, hugging the little girl to her chest.

Deedra reached outstretched hands toward the toddler. "That woman has my child, Heck. My Callie."

"She's loco," the woman said. "Plumb nuts. This is my granddaughter."

"Ms. Shanahan." Heck stepped between the women. "You got it wrong. This here is Luanne Pine's mama. And the little girl is Luanne's daughter, Jess."

Only then did the weeping child lift its head from the woman's shoulder and turn tear-damp eyes at Deedra. Brown eyes.

It was not Callie.

Deedra's knees gave out.

Before she hit the floor she felt Beau's strong hands catch her, heard his voice call her name. But all she could think was that once again she'd let him down. Once again she'd lost Callie.

Chapter Ten

"Where were you, Beau?" Deedra murmured against his chest. "Where were you?"

Beau held her trembling body as tightly as he could without hurting her. She clung to him, pressing her face to his chest as if she wanted to disappear into him. What the hell had happened? Over the top of her head, he glanced from Heck Long to the chubby woman with the child, silently gesturing for one or both to start explaining.

When neither accommodated, he barked, "What happened? Why is Deedra covered in—" he sniffed "—baby powder?"

"I don't know." Heck shrugged. "She came runnin' in here after Luanne's mama, claimin' Jess was your Callie."

Beau blanched, his gaze swinging to the little girl. Except for the shoulder-length wavy black hair, she didn't look anything like Callie. His chest tightened, and he drew a difficult breath. Like Callie would look now, that is, at two years old. Besides, this child was more like three. God, what had set Dee off? He stroked her back. "I'm sorry, Mrs., er..."

He realized he didn't know Luanne's mother's name.

The woman supplied it. "Lowry. Ivy Lowry."

Luanne had a perfect oval face, but her mother's had lost all definition to fat and was mottled and red, a testament to the claim that she'd been running. Ivy had gray-streaked, coffee-brown hair in a short, mannish cut. Her aqua eyes peered at Beau over half glasses embedded with multicolored rhinestones, one of which was missing on the left side.

He said again, "I'm sorry, Mrs. Lowry."

"She scared us half to death, Sheriff." Ivy shook a finger at Deedra. "Chased us all the way from Dupont's Department Store."

"We lost our little girl six months ago. Callie had hair a lot like Jess's." Beau hugged Deedra reassuringly. "My wife is having a hard time—"

"Ah, poor thing. Well, no wonder she acted plumb loco." Ivy's eyes softened, and pity etched lines into her fleshy face. "Lord knows what I'd do if someone took one of my girls from me. Make 'em sorrier than they'd ever been, for sure. Yeah, I might go off my rocker, too."

"I'm not off my rocker," Deedra said, lifting her head from Beau's shoulder. She glanced around at Mrs. Lowry. "No trace of her was ever found—which is probably why I'm having trouble accepting that she's…gone."

"It don't do no good to dwell on stuff like that, Ms. Shanahan," Heck offered. "You gotta cut yerself a break."

"Yeah. Let's just forget the whole thing, okay, hon?" Mrs. Lowry sounded as if she'd never forget it. As if she couldn't wait to tell everyone she knew about her first meeting with the sheriff's wife.

"Thank you, Mrs. Lowry. Your discretion would

mean a lot to me.'' Beau pinned her with his toughest gaze, hoping she'd take the hint and keep her mouth shut. For his sake, for the sake of this office and for Luanne's sake. He was, after all, Luanne's boss, and he wouldn't appreciate his employee and her family making fun of his wife behind his back.

''Oh, my lord, my packages!'' Ivy Lowry clapped her hand on her cheek. ''I dropped 'em right out there on the street.''

With that, she gathered up Jess and fled.

Deedra stepped back from Beau. Her complexion rivaled the shade of the powder in her hair and on her clothes. ''Beau, I—''

''Come into my office.'' She was still trembling. But given the distress and terror she'd been through the last few days, it wasn't that strange that she'd be in shock. He nodded to his deputy. ''Heck, bring us some of that mud you call coffee.''

He guided Deedra into his office and shut the door, then closed the blinds, giving them complete privacy. Other than a few pink phone messages, there was no work on his desk. He hitched his hip on its edge. Deedra dropped into a chair facing him and buried her head in her hands. She wasn't weeping—though God knows she had reason. She seemed more ashamed, somehow worried that he'd be upset with her. ''Dee, what happened?''

She lifted her head. ''You heard that…Mrs. Lowry. I thought her granddaughter was…Callie.''

''But why? What made you think Callie is alive?''

''You mean…what threw me 'off my rocker'?''

He stroked her cheek, wanting to pull her closer and ease the pain from her dove-gray eyes. ''I wouldn't put it that way.''

"You'd be the only one." She blew out a breath but remained tense.

"Sweetheart, I just want to know what happened after I left you at the doctor's?"

"Nothing happened. Nothing concrete, anyway. It was a series of things, I guess. My doctor's visit, an encounter with a pregnant teenager and an adopting couple—all started me thinking about babies, which of course led to thoughts of Callie, and next thing I knew I was in the infant department of Dupont's smelling the baby powder, remembering... And then, a swatch of green on a sale rack caught my eye."

She lifted her gaze, pleading for his understanding. "It was the dress Callie was wearing—"

"Callie's dress?" Shock scraped Beau's nerves. "Her actual dress?"

"No...no...just one like it."

His heart kicked, a painful, unpleasant bump that seemed to shove something solid into his throat. "Oh, God, oh, babe..."

She shuddered and hugged herself, swallowing so hard he thought she'd choke. He caught her by both hands, and she gripped back until her knuckles were white.

Unshed tears shone in her eyes. "I felt as if I stood half on and half off the edge of a bottomless pit, felt my body pitching over that rim, and I couldn't pull back. Couldn't stop the forward momentum. The little girl's laugh did that. Snapped me back to reality. It sounded like Callie's laugh, and when I turned and saw that raven hair...well, you know the rest."

"Ah, Dee, I'm sorry." He gently brushed her hair, sending white dust into the air. "How did you get the baby powder all over you?"

She told him about not realizing she still held the talcum can when she'd started for the little girl, about slamming into the shelf and spilling everything, including herself and the powder. "God, Beau. The whole town is going to be talking about how I flipped out in Dupont's. Uncle Sean will be mortified. Hell, I'm mortified."

She looked so contrite, so dismayed, he caught her face in both hands, forced her gaze to his and said with conviction, "Sean and the town will get over it."

The deputy knocked on the door, then opened it and came in with two cups of steaming coffee. He set them on Beau's desk. "Sheriff, Dr. Warren is on line one. I told her you were busy, but she insists it's important."

"Dr. Warren?" Deedra flinched.

Beau stiffened. "Tell the doctor that I'll call her back when I'm free."

Heck nodded and left.

"I suppose *she's* heard already." Deedra groaned. "And wants to recommend you have me committed before I hurt myself or someone else."

"Forget Dr. Warren. I think we're on the same page about your *former* shrink." Beau poured brandy into each of their mugs. He handed her one. "Here, this will make you feel better."

He drank from his own cup. "Now, what did Dr. Haynes say about your surgery?"

She sipped at the steamy brew, then peered at him over the rim of the mug. "Scheduled for six weeks from now. That gives me time to save up my own blood."

He scowled, thinking about the blood that had been switched in that hospital in Washington State.

As though she'd read his mind, she added, "Dr.

Haynes knows, and he's guaranteed me he'll find some way to keep my blood under lock and key, even if he has to store it in his own home.''

Beau wasn't convinced that would keep the sniper from trying to sabotage it. They had to find out who she was. And fast. He finished his coffee, shoved his phone messages unread into his top drawer and struggled up, relying heavily on his cane. *Damned physical therapist.* His leg hadn't bothered him this morning, but after their impromptu session today, it hurt like hell. He needed to get off his feet, and Deedra looked as done in as he felt. "Come on. Let's go home."

Deedra stood, and he took her arm. The outer office was empty again.

"Why didn't you come and pick me up?" Deedra asked. "Where were you, Beau? Did it have something to do with the page you got at Dr. Haynes?"

"No. That was from Nora Lee. She wanted me to know the forensics team had finished up, and we could have our bedroom and bathroom back.''

"Then what delayed you?"

"My physical therapist called. He had a cancellation, so I took it. Unfortunately, it lasted longer than I'd counted on, and by the time I called Dr. Haynes you'd already gone.''

They had just reached Beau's car when a woman called his name. "Sheriff Shanahan?"

Dr. Elle Warren bore down on them, her compact body oozing energy and strength like a finely tuned machine. As usual she wore a suit with a leotard and tennis shoes looking gym-ready should anyone suggest working out. "Sheriff, I really need to speak to you." She eyed Deedra critically. "Alone."

Bristling, Beau led Deedra to the passenger side of

the car. She settled on the seat and he gently closed the door. Only then, did he address the shrink. "Didn't my deputy inform you that I'd call you back?"

"Yes, but considering the…delicacy of this matter, I decided we should discuss it in person." Her long, sandy hair was swept off her forehead and secured at the nape, as controlled as the woman herself. Always in charge, always in command. "Could we please go into your office?"

As though he would follow her, Dr. Warren took a step toward the precinct.

Beau addressed the psychologist's back. "I'm busy right now."

Dr. Warren glanced around, seeming surprised. Not used to having her requests ignored, he imagined. She touched a small hand to her hair. "I only need a few minutes."

"Right now I don't have them to spare." He opened his car door. "I'll call you tomorrow."

"But—"

"Tomorrow." He drove off, leaving the shrink on the street, hands on hips, chest heaving, face twisted and red. But Deedra was smiling.

DEEDRA KEPT SMILING, all the way home, all the way up to their bedroom. Thanks to Beau. He'd done what she'd prayed for before she'd run away. He'd actually been there for her at her worst moment, supported her through her most difficult hour. For the first time since this ordeal had started, she felt they were a team.

"Thank you."

He shook his head and blinked down at her. "For what?"

"For riding to my rescue today."

"Yeah, I'm a regular white knight."

"You were, Beau. To me." She reached up, stroked his face, wound her fingers into his hair and then pulled him to her. She raised on tiptoe to meet his kiss, their lips coming together in hunger, hard and demanding. Electrical zings jolted through her, kicking her heartbeat into overdrive and shooting fireworks through her veins.

He seemed to feel it, too. The cane dropped near their feet, and he rocked back against the door, dragging her to him, his arms circling her like bands of unbreakable silk. Deedra's body felt boneless. His tongue parted her lips, and the moment she tasted him, she knew she could never get enough of Beau.

Beau pulled back, breathless, his gaze glazed with want. "I won't hurt you. Last night I didn't think about your condition…but I've been worried about it all day. Did…did our lovemaking cause you any…harm? What did the doctor say?"

She couldn't catch her breath. "You sure know how to kill a moment."

"Deedra?" His husky whisper vibrated along her nerve endings as his exploring hands rolled the length of her back, settling on her bottom, pulling her near enough that she had no doubt he was still up for the activity he had put on hold. "What did the doctor say?"

"He said we could…if we go easy. As long as I don't start to bleed." She feared the clinical intrusion would dampen the mood, but he grinned lustily and grabbed her lips with his, delving into her mouth. Then he kissed her face, her neck, her forehead as if he couldn't get enough of her…until her body seemed to be burning from the inside out.

Her internal thermometer spiked, spreading a candied ache through her. A roaring need. They began undressing each other, all the while sharing kisses, touches, caresses, the wildfire roaring higher, the need coiling tighter.

And then they were naked, skin to skin, as giddy as children in a candy store, gazes locked on all the goodies, not sure which delight to sample first. This one, then this, then this. Each one more delicious than the last. And she was melting again, against his tongue, against his fingertips, against his glances. Without knowing how, she felt the bed beneath her. Beau knelt above her, between her legs, the pièce de résistance, the most coveted goody in the store, the sweetest treat of all.

He entered her with a thrust so gentle, if not for the sheer size of him and her body's immediate and shattering response, she might have thought she'd imagined their joining. Radiant currents zipped through her, thrilled her, and she urged him deeper and deeper. He accommodated, shoved all the way in, then stilled, savoring the moment, driving her mad with the urgency for what he withheld, frantic for that which he would not give.

"Beau, please. Please," she begged, gyrating her hips against his. He groaned, and she sighed in satisfaction.

"Deedra…?" His emerald eyes were jade with ardor, his voice ragged, "Are you sure?"

"Oh, yes." She sighed. "Very sure."

"Hallelujah!" He moved then, his thrusts still schooled, but every lift and dip heightened the exquisite friction, winding the coil inside her tighter and tighter until the spring snapped loose in a wild backlash that soared through her, carrying her as high and as far as the universe allowed.

Beau cried her name and clung to her, and Deedra closed her eyes, feeling a new contentment. They'd survived the storm. This time. They could go on to fight another day. To face the next bluster bearing down on them. But for now it was enough to just lie here in his embrace, snug in the afterglow.

She came back to herself sometime later with no idea how late it was or how long they'd slept. But it was still light outside and Beau was still asleep.

She went into the bathroom to shower. The air smelled of lemon-scented cleanser, and she silently thanked Pilar for being fastidious and cleaning up after the forensics unit and Nora Lee. Stretching, she realized she felt good. Almost her old self. Trouble was, she decided, studying her reflection, she didn't look like herself. She couldn't do anything about the weight loss at the moment, but there was something she could make right.

She dug into her travel bag and withdrew a box of hair dye. Within the hour she had her own russet hair back, and the color changed the woman in the glass in every way for the better. Her gray eyes had depth and definition again, her complexion its normal peachy hue. She grinned. "Welcome back, Deedra."

"I'll second that," Beau said, eyeing her with lusty approval. "You look good enough to haul back to bed, lady."

He kissed her neck, and a sweet heat began claiming her.

It was cut off by a loud banging on their bedroom door.

"Are you two coming down for supper or not?" Sean barked.

Beau and Deedra exchanged a knowing glance. Her breath shuddered out; her nerves burned beneath her skin. She said, "He's heard about the incident at Dupont's."

"Probably." Beau nodded. "Give us half an hour, okay, Sean?"

"I've already given you an hour." Sean tempered his voice, but not his annoyance. "And I'm gettin' damned hungry."

"Make it ten minutes then."

"But no more."

"So much for my plans, babe," Beau said, kissing her again.

While he showered, she dressed, then took special care with her makeup, needing to look strong, unshaken.

Needing a shield against Sean's anger.

What she'd done today likely only accounted for part of his ire. She didn't like that she was coming between Beau and his uncle. After Beau's parents died, Sean and Beau had become more than uncle and nephew. More like father and son. Or older and younger brothers—considering that the gap in their ages wasn't all that great.

Sean had adored Callie. Had never gotten over her loss. Deedra knew he was terrified she would somehow cost him Beau, and he was reacting with the only weapon left in his arsenal. His temper.

A leaden band circled her chest, squeezing her heart in a vise-grip of sorrow. Sean didn't hate her; he distrusted her. From their first meeting he'd recognized in her the fatal flaw that Beau had never seen: she couldn't trust love enough to give her whole heart to anyone. Even with Callie, she'd held back. Just in case her daughter would find her lacking. Would leave her. Or be taken from her.

And hadn't that been exactly what happened? It was that emotional distancing that lay at the root of her guilt about the accident. About her baby's disappearance.

Ten minutes to the second, she and Beau descended the stairs. He seemed as tense as she, as if he were ready to take on the world—should the need arise. The realization saddened her. Dinner in one's own home shouldn't be a battleground, but a comfortable place to enjoy the fruits of daily labor, the company of loved ones. Beau's tension reinforced her conviction that she was pulling this family apart. In her experience, once that kind of fissure began nothing could heal it.

But maybe she could slow it down a bit.

The aroma of something spicy stole through the lower level, guiding them toward the dining room. Sean was already seated, napkin tucked into the collar of his crisp chambray shirt like a baby's bib. Her baby's bib. Pilar bustled into the room and set hot plates on trivets. She didn't glance at Deedra. Obviously, she had also heard about Dupont's.

Deedra decided to defuse the situation, if possible. "It smells delicious, Pilar. I'm sorry we kept you both waiting."

Sean only grunted, but the apology took the housekeeper by surprise. She acknowledged it with a small smile and thanked Deedra. "Oh, my. You fix hair color. I like."

Even Sean gave his grudging approval.

Deedra forced a smile and lifted her fork, but she had no appetite. She couldn't sit in this room without seeing Callie in her high chair. Of course the high chair had been removed, but the memory couldn't be carried out of her head and stored in the shed. Nor could what she'd done this afternoon, what she'd felt.

For a few hours today she'd allowed Beau to pull her out of herself, to push away the day's events. She hadn't had to examine how easily she'd fallen into believing that Callie lived. But the reprieve had run out. She spent the next half hour moving her food around on her plate and mulling over the incident in Dupont's. That she could so easily buy into Callie being alive and well, hidden somewhere in this small town…that she could so easily abandon her own sanity, terrified her. One way or another she had to accept her daughter's death. Or she'd lose her mind.

And Beau.

After the meal Sean asked Beau to stay and join him for a glass of whiskey. Deedra didn't like leaving Beau to explain her behavior to his uncle, but he insisted. In the kitchen she helped Pilar put away the leftovers and load the dishwasher. The task seemed exhausting, and she realized it wasn't the kitchen chores that had zapped her energy, but the letting go, at long last, of the hope that Callie lived. The sense she'd had of feeling good earlier was gone. She wanted nothing more at the moment than to crawl into bed and let Beau hold her, comfort her, grieve with her.

She bade Pilar good-night and shuffled into the hallway. Cigar smoke floated on the air. Catching her name coming from the dining room, she hesitated. Had one of the men called to her? She started to answer, then heard Sean say, ''…Deedra let you think she might be dead, son. For two months. That ain't right thinkin'.''

"Someone was trying to kill her," Beau said. "Is still trying to kill her."

"Why? What's she done that someone wants her dead? Have you asked her that?"

"It has nothing to do with Dee. But with me."

"You? Someone you put in jail or somethin'?"

"It's too much to go into right now."

"Hell's bells, boy, she comes waltzin' back in here, crookin' her finger and leadin' you around like a little puppy dog. Comes a time a man needs to think with his brains and not with what's stirrin' in his pants."

"That's enough, Sean." Beau's chair scraped back on the hardwood floor.

"You shoulda hooked up with Cassidy," Sean said. "She's as easy on the eyes as they come, and she'd give you some big, scrappin' sons to carry on the Shanahan name."

As though he'd stuck a knife hilt-deep into her very soul, Deedra stumbled back, pain radiating the length of her. She fled to the stairs, her heart shriveling in her chest. She'd lost the only baby she could ever give Beau. There would be no "big, scrappin' sons," no Shanahan heirs as long as he stayed married to her. Beau would be the end of his line. The last of the Shanahan clan. For Beau that would be as big a tragedy as losing Callie had been.

As if lightning had slashed before her eyes, shattering the warm illusions of the afternoon with Beau, she suffered a stunning realization. She swayed with the shock. Though she hadn't consciously given her heart to Beau, he'd laid claim to it. All of it. *Oh, God, help me.* The pounding against her ribs felt as if the vital organ in question was trying to escape from her chest. She loved Beau. Loved him with every ounce of her being. Loved him so much she could not allow him to go through his life without being a father, without the family he deserved, without "scrappin' sons" and more daughters.

She loved him enough to give him up.

She jammed her fists against the tears filling her eyes. No. She wouldn't cry. Wouldn't feel sorry for herself. Wouldn't let Beau see or guess the depth of her distress. She hugged herself against the heartache. Her back began to throb.

She was just swallowing two of her pills when Beau arrived.

"There you are," he said, grinning like a child delighted to see its favorite toy.

Her pulse skipped faster at the sight of him, too. An unbidden smile sprang to her lips. He was the most gorgeous man she'd ever laid eyes on, a visual pleasure to behold, but that was merely the shell. The inner man was the beautiful one, the one who had stolen her heart, branded her soul. He'd done it with such gentleness, such ingenuousness, he'd taken her unaware.

"You feeling okay?" Concern narrowed his green eyes as he studied her. "You look kind of pale."

"It's nothing." *I was just thinking about Callie. And you.* She left the bathroom light on, but doused the bedroom lights and threw open the French doors to the balcony, welcoming the soft breeze of tepid evening air against her face. The night was dark, moonless, and she could barely make out the wrought-iron furniture on the deck. Aware that the light behind them made them perfect targets for the sniper, she hovered at the jamb, safe in the shadows of the bedroom.

Beau came up behind her. "God, but I've missed

you. I want to drag you back to bed and show you how much.''

He smelled of whiskey, cigar and the special scent that was his alone and that always drew her to him even though she knew she should resist, especially now that she knew she'd soon be leaving for good. But her skin shivered where he kissed her neck and future heartache seemed light-years away.

But she was wrong. As she leaned back into him, the bedside phone rang. Shrill and demanding, it startled Deedra, though she couldn't say why.

Chapter Eleven

The day-care house in Butte looked like an exploded toy box. Stuffed animals, dolls, tricycles, rainbow-hued buckets and tiny trucks were strewn from one end of the yard to the other. But the favorite was the over-turned wagon with the bunny sprawled beside it.

Just the way Callie Shanahan's bunny had sprawled beside the overturned Jeep.

Too bad Deedra hadn't died in that damned accident. She should have. She'd seemed to be slipping away. Her pulse all but impossible to find. If someone hadn't come along so soon, time would have finished her off. Or one of the nocturnal predators drawn by the scent of her blood.

Then Beau Shanahan's misery would have been complete.

Then his wife wouldn't have run away to Washington and made it necessary to silence the loose end hiding inside this damned daycare. The way her son had been silenced. Waiting for darkness had fried nerves already seared with impatience. But once it began its descent, night came quick and black.

The sniper pulled the pistol from the glovebox and added the silencer. No rifle for this kill. It would be up close and personal. Face-to-face. The old woman had to pay for the days wasted watching the house to determine whether she was there or not.

But for all the old lady's precautions—no lights, no smoke from the chimney, no taking out of the garbage, no trips to the grocers—she'd finally made a fatal mistake and peeked out from behind the curtain of an upper window. Finally shown her pinched and frightened face.

Foolish crone thought hiding in the trilevel would keep her safe. The sniper smirked and patted a front pants pocket, fingers grazing the bump of metal there. Nell Carter's spare house key. It had been easily located. Her phone easily monitored. ''Thank you, God, for spy technology.''

Amazingly the old gal hadn't called the police about the woman who'd come looking for her son. But she would. Eventually. The sniper slammed the clip into the gun; the accompanying clink seemed loud inside the cab of the pickup. Louder than the shot would be.

Five feet ahead a streetlight came on giving the sniper pause, even though precautions had been taken. The windows of the truck were blacked out, making seeing into the cab all but impossible. The license plates wore a coating of mud that obscured the numbers. Of course, there was always the unexpected—say, a neighbor noticing the truck didn't belong to any of the residents on this street and calling the cops. It seemed a minor concern, though, given most of the neighborhood pushed seventy and retired before dark.

The sniper groped for the Dupont's shopping bag between the bucket seats. Its paper crackle was reassuring, and it roused the memory of Deedra falling apart today in the department store. The sniper laughed with glee.

Couldn't have orchestrated her descent into emotional hell better myself. Vengeance was proving to be sweeter than expected.

The telephone-listening device beeped, breaking the jolly mood. Beau Shanahan's home number appeared on the readout. So, the little mouse in the hole had finally found her nerve. "It's showtime."

The door of the pickup slipped open. The sniper stepped out, gun in pants waistband. The Dupont's sack held tight. Inside the shopping bag: a nasty surprise for Deedra.

Chapter Twelve

Deedra hurried to answer the phone. "Hello?"

"Deedra? Is that you?"

The woman spoke so quietly she didn't recognize the voice.

"Yes."

"It's me, Nell Carter."

Oh, God, Nell. She'd forgotten to tell Beau about her urgent messages. He was staring at her now, wanting to know who it was.

"I saw you at my house the other day," Nell said. "I'm sorry I didn't answer the door. I just couldn't."

A wealth of guilt hit Deedra. She should have called Nell before this. Sent flowers. Gone back to visit her after hearing about Freddie's murder. Should have made sure Beau called her back sometime today. She started to offer her condolences.

Nell cut her off. "I need to speak with your husband. Right now."

Beau mouthed, Who is it?

Deedra placed her hand over the receiver. "Freddie's mom."

He nodded and signaled that he'd leave her alone to talk in private.

She caught his arm. "No, Beau. Don't go. She wants to talk to you."

"Me?" He arched an eyebrow, totally puzzled. He could not imagine any subject Freddie Carter's mother would have to discuss with him. He'd never met her. "Why?"

"She didn't tell me." Deedra shrugged. "But I know she left you two urgent messages today at the office."

"Huh?" He thought of the phone messages he'd shoved unread into his desk drawer. "I didn't get to my messages…"

"And…I forgot to tell you." Deedra's cheeks reddened. She handed him the receiver and sank wearily to the bed.

He lifted the phone to his ear. "Mrs. Carter, Beau Shanahan. What can I do for you?"

"That remains to be seen." Her voice was as delicate as a bird's cheep. "Without all the children here every day, making so much noise a body can't hear her own thoughts, I've had nothing to do but think."

"About what?" Rubbing his leg, he eased onto the bed beside Deedra. She was listening, he noted, to his end of the conversation with rapt curiosity.

"About my Freddie being run down by that van driver. And now I don't think it was random."

"You don't?"

"No."

"And you think you know why?"

"Maybe."

"Have you presented your theory to the police officer on Freddie's case?"

"He isn't interested, and I'm not going to beg anyone to hear me out. All those cops ever did was hassle my Freddie and his father before him.''

"So, do you want to tell me?"

She didn't answer. There was a pause as if she were drawing in on a cigarette. "I started asking myself why, why Freddie?"

Myriad reasons popped into Beau's mind. Freddie Carter had spent his life conning the unsuspecting. Any of his dupes might have sought revenge. But listing motives to his grieving mother would be cruel. Beau kept silent. "Do you think you know why?"

"You tell me."

His eyebrows and his interest stirred. "I beg your pardon?"

"I figure it might have something to do with why Deedra went missing."

He glanced at his wife, his chest tightening at the reminder of that awful time, at the realization that she was about as unstable now as she'd been then. He rubbed his leg harder as if to ease the residual pain in his heart and the immediate ache in his calf. "Why would you think that?"

"About a week before he was run down, a woman came here looking to find Freddie. He told me later that she'd paid him a nice bit of change for information on Deedra's whereabouts."

Beau's pulse stumbled, and he stopped stroking his leg. "So, Freddie did tell this woman where to find Deedra?"

Beside him, Deedra sat straight up, her eyes rounding. He felt sure she had already accepted Freddie's betrayal, but the confirmation had to wound her. He caught her hand and squeezed it.

Nell said, "Yes, he did, and since Deedra is home now, I'm assuming the woman found her."

"Sort of." Beau's guts started to tighten.

"You know, at the time, I figured you'd hired the woman." There was another pause and then an exhale like smoke being blown out. "I remember thinking she must be a private investigator or maybe a bounty hunter, since she was driving a pickup truck with one of those gun racks in the window."

Beau's pulse stumbled, his grip on Deedra's hand tightening. "You saw her truck?"

"Yes." Nell took another puff. "I'm sorry that my Freddie helped Deedra disappear."

"What kind of truck was she driving?"

"He was a good son, Mr. Shanahan. But he never got over Deedra marrying you. I think he loved her, but she didn't love him the same way. He started hating her in the end. It was the drink. I never thought he'd end up a boozer like his father, but he did."

"Mrs. Carter. Did you get a good look at the truck? Could you describe it?"

"Maybe. Though I don't know one make or model from another. But I need to know a few more things before we go into that." She drew on her cigarette. "Mr. Shanahan, if it's not too personal, will you please tell me why Deedra found it necessary to go away and not tell anyone, except Freddie, where she'd be?"

"Someone is trying to kill her." Beau struggled to keep the urgency and frustration out of his voice, until it hit him that Nell needed a jolt of reality. She needed to know how dangerous the evidence she possessed might be. "Perhaps the same someone who killed your son."

"Then, I don't suppose you sent this woman to Freddie, did you?"

"No."

There was a chilling silence on her end.

"The woman," Beau said, struggling to his feet, excitement ripping through him as he balanced on his cane. "Did she give you a name?"

Nell laughed, a sharp sarcastic chirp. "Not likely it'd be her real one if she's a killer, right?"

"Just the same, if you remember who she said she was, I need to know." His pulse hammered against his temples.

"Oh, I remember the name she used. Who wouldn't? It sounded made up at the time and then I realized why. It was the name of a former first lady. Nancy Davis Reagan. You know any woman with that name?"

"No." He was only mildly disappointed. He might not have a name, but he had an eyewitness. "Can you describe her?"

"My eyes aren't what they used to be, but I'm not blind."

Excitement poured through his limbs. He covered the receiver and told Deedra to dig the tablet and pen from the nightstand. As soon as she had the pen poised over a blank page, he said, "Okay, Mrs. Carter, go ahead."

"You don't understand. You've confirmed my worst fears. I thought maybe I was being paranoid these past few days. Thought maybe that really wasn't her truck I've seen cruising past the house. But now I know it is. I don't want her to know I'm here. I haven't dared go out. I'm running out of food. I can't risk having anything delivered. I don't dare turn on a lamp. Or the TV. Why do you think I'm speaking so low to you?"

He'd thought her voice birdlike, but understood now that she was talking just above a whisper. He felt sudden fear for her. "Then describe her and the truck to me and—"

"Oh, my God. There it is."

Alarm shot through Beau. "What color is the pickup, Mrs. Carter?"

"It's parked two houses down."

"We're on our way. Keep the doors locked and stay out of sight."

But the line had gone dead.

Beau hung up, adrenaline pumping through his veins. He told Deedra the gist of what he'd learned as he dialed Nora Lee's cell phone and listened to it ring. She finally answered. He filled her in and told her what he wanted. "I know it's late, but we need to do this tonight. ASAP."

"It's okay, Sheriff. I'm at my Mom's, just outside of Butte, but I've got my charcoals and sketch pad with me. Give me the address and I'll meet you there."

"Be quick about it. I have a feeling we need to get there pronto."

Beau hurried to the wall safe and did something he hadn't done since he'd been shot by Mann: strapped on a gun.

"I'm going with you," Deedra said, racing to the closet for shoes and a coat.

He lifted his Stetson. "No, Dee. There's only one way to get there quickly."

She stiffened. *The shortcut.* It would mean they'd be passing the site of her accident with Callie. "Through the woods."

"Yes."

She crammed her arms into her jacket. Yes, she'd

fallen apart today, but somehow tonight she felt something like steel in her very core. Maybe revisiting the accident site, even briefly, was the final step in accepting her daughter's death. Once she saw that it was nothing more monstrous than a dirt road, a passage that led travelers from one place to another, it would no longer haunt her nightmares. She grabbed her purse. "If you can take it, so can I."

"Are you sure?"

She knew he couldn't deal with two distressed females at the same time; Freddie's mother would be enough. "Nell knows me. She trusts me. She may open up easier for you if I'm there."

"I think we should bring her back here for protection, Dee. She can stay in one of the guest rooms."

The offer was so generous and so much like the Beau she'd fallen in love with, she planted a quick kiss on his cheek and preceded him down the stairs.

Minutes later the car tore through the woods. It was still daylight, but here the trees grew so close together it was necessary to turn on the headlights. The beams bounced off the pines, which jumped at them in startling flashes like dancing goblins. Deedra gripped the edge of the seat, grappling with her shaky nerves. The car careened along, faster and faster. The tires hitting the dirt road like a chant, *Callie! Callie! Callie!*

"Are you okay?" Beau asked.

She heard the husky note in his voice, knew this drive was no easier for him than it was for her. She embraced that inner steel rod, clinging to it like a support post on a subway train roaring toward hell. "I'm fine."

But even as she said it, she saw the start of the S curve ahead. The car slowed to a safer speed, but to

Deedra it crawled, moving in slow motion, every rotation of the wheel spiraling her backward to the day of her accident. It had been a warm afternoon. Branches occasionally brushed the Jeep's roll bars. Callie sat beside her, strapped into her protective seat, the soles of her Mary Janes smeared with the red barn paint she'd stepped in two days earlier.

A favorite Faith Hill song blasted out of the speakers. From the time she could walk, Callie had expressed an enjoyment of music, her feet keeping beat. That day she was even singing along. Not the actual words or tune, but her own rendition full of the few words she spoke and a jumble of baby talk.

As the memory resurfaced, Deedra smiled, welcoming it. To better hear her little girl, she'd reached over to turn down the CD player and at the same time tapped the brakes. It took a moment for her to realize she had no brakes. The panic she'd felt then hit her now, stripping her smile.

Then the screen in her mind went black, all memory of the accident cut off like a snapped piece of film. She couldn't recall anything beyond the fear of realizing the brakes didn't work. She'd thought coming to the site would bring it back. It hadn't. It didn't.

Her doctor had warned she might never remember.

All she knew was what she'd been told once she was recovering. The Jeep had no air bags. On impact with the felled tree, the vehicle had flipped, driver's side down. Her head had slammed into the tree trunk so hard she'd been knocked out immediately. A sharp branch had stabbed her chest, missing her heart by inches. She'd remained unconscious until after she'd come out of surgery.

She blinked and looked at the woods that had swallowed all trace of her daughter with the finality of a depraved deity receiving a sacrificial virgin. Deedra felt no sign of her, no sense that Callie lived. She'd thought if Callie had survived, was out there waiting to be found, Deedra would feel it here more than anywhere else. But she felt only grief and loss, and in that instant she finally accepted that Callie was gone.

Forever.

Tears filled her eyes and her heart and crowded into her very soul. She covered her mouth, holding in a sob. They'd been given a precious gift, not for as long as they'd have chosen, but for as long as God had allotted. Instead of moping around, thinking she saw Callie in every black-haired little girl she encountered, she had to let her go. Let her find eternal peace.

She sniffed, sucking back the sorrow. She didn't have the luxury of falling apart now. Callie was beyond her help, but Nell knew who was responsible for her loss. With that knowledge, they could end this nightmare. Could finally lay Callie to rest. She focused on that.

"Are you all right?" Beau asked again, concern defining his tone.

"I will be." But would she? In one evening she'd had to accept the death of her daughter and the inevitable split from this man she loved. Sorrow settled in her chest like a block of ice.

He caught her hand, then hit the gas harder as the road straightened. For a long moment she held on to him, sensing that he was also remembering the little girl who had sealed their love, who'd filled their lives with such joy, who would be forever missed. As the wooded area thinned and began to fall away, Deedra felt herself letting go, of Callie and of Beau's hand.

She wasn't ready to release him completely. Couldn't deal with that loss tonight. She forced her mind elsewhere, to Nell, and her heart filled with a different kind of chill. Nell was in danger because of her. *Because I came to Freddie for help, because I trusted him one time too many.*

On the main route to Butte, Beau employed the tools of his trade; red and blue lights strobed against the darkening sky and the siren bleated with the sense of urgency coursing through Deedra's veins.

Please, don't let anything happen to Nell… Please. But even as she prayed, she knew this heartless killer didn't operate under God's will. Not the person who'd run down Freddie, who'd coldly switched the blood in that Washington hospital and caused the death of that innocent surgery patient. Not the person who'd left an eighteen-month-old to crawl into a wilderness full of natural predators. Prayers couldn't touch that kind of evil.

The sudden silence snapped Deedra out of her dark reverie. Beau had shut off the siren and doused the overhead lights. They were entering Nell's neighborhood. Her muscles tightened.

Beau slowed the car to a crawl. "If the driver of that pickup is still parked down the street, I don't want to warn her of our presence."

He drove the length of Nell's street and back, but the only pickup on the whole block belonged to Nora Lee Anderson. Parked in front of the day care, it was one of those three-door trucks with a bench seat behind the front two buckets. In the glow cast by the street light, Deedra couldn't make out the color. Something light. White or beige or maybe yellow. "Did Nell tell you the color of the pickup?"

"No, dammit. She hung up before I could get it out of her. But don't go thinking it's one of my deputies." He nodded toward Nora Lee's truck. "She was having dinner at her mother's when I called her."

Nora Lee sat behind the wheel, but opened her door the moment they pulled to a stop. She stepped out, raising a hand to shield her pale blue eyes against the glare of Beau's headlights. She wore white jeans and a white T-shirt rolled up her muscular arms. A Nordic hellcat. A poster girl for white supremacist recruiting.

She carried a case that Deedra assumed held her sketch pad and charcoal pencils. "I didn't approach the house, Sheriff. Figured I'd better wait for you since the subject wouldn't be expecting me."

"Good thinking, Nora Lee. Did you happen to see a pickup truck parked a couple of houses down when you arrived?"

"No. And I perused the street the way you did when I got here."

"Okay." Beau closed his door as quietly as possible. "You hear anything from the forensics lab yet?"

"It's too soon. The tech told me that it would be a few days even with a rush on it. They're pretty slammed. But I dusted both rooms and the rental car and didn't find any strange prints, just yours, Ms. Shanahan's and Pilar's. So it's likely the unsub wore gloves."

Even though this was what they'd expected, Deedra felt a touch of disappointment. Maybe the lab would have better luck. Beau went through the gate first, its eerie squeak like a finger on a blackboard. Deedra trailed behind Nora Lee. In the moonless night, the sunny yellow trilevel loomed large and murky. The toys littering the yard seemed as if they'd gone undisturbed since they'd been here earlier in the week. She started up the walk and bumped against the wagon. It lay on its side, the bunny sprawled beside it the same way Callie's bunny had appeared in the police photos. Her gaze locked on the floppy-eared toy. What had happened to Callie's bunny? Had Beau brought it home? Stored it in the shed with the rest of her things? Or had the toy, the last thing his daughter had held, been too painful for him to handle?

She started to dip down to pick up this bunny, but Beau caught her elbow. "It's not hers, Dee."

She blanched and straightened, allowing him to escort her past the offensive toys to the porch. She stumbled along beside him, noticing how dark and still the house appeared. The drapes drawn. No light peeking from within. "You'd think she'd be on the lookout for us, would have seen us arrive and been here to greet us."

Beau didn't answer, but tension limned off him like a luminous shadow. His big fist struck the door. "Mrs. Carter, it's Beau Shanahan."

When she didn't answer, he repeated himself, hollered this time. His shout echoed off the porch, startlingly loud on the subdued street.

Deedra felt her worse fears coming true. "Oh, God." She moved past Beau and tried the knob. "It's locked. But I know where she hides a key in back. Come on."

Fear hurried her down the steps, but moving through the minefield of fallen toys wasted precious minutes. The backyard had a swing set and a play house. A flower bed circled the toy home. A cluster of ceramic frogs of varying sizes and colors nestled to one side of it. "The key is under the biggest frog. The fat red one."

Beau steadied his flashlight beam on the garden frog, lifted it, and searched the flower bed where it had sat. "There's no key here."

Deedra's heart pumped so hard it started to ache. "Maybe it's under one of the other frogs."

Beau turned over the cluster one by one. "Nope."

"God, Beau, what if the sniper found it and..." She choked on the horror of her own imagination.

"Stay here, Dee. Out of sight." He handed her the flashlight, shutting off the beam. "Keep it turned off. Hide in the darkness."

He withdrew the gun from his holster and clicked off the safety. "You got your weapon, Nora Lee?"

"Right here." She pulled it from the leather art bag, dropped the bag to the grass and followed Beau.

He told her, "Keep my back."

The two police officers raced to the kitchen door, disappearing from Deedra's sight. A second later Beau shouted, "Nell! Police! Coming in!"

In the next instant came a dark and ominous quiet. Nothing stirred. Except the hair on Deedra's nape. She'd never felt so vulnerable as she did at that moment, alone in the backyard all but invisible under cover of the moonless night.

But was she alone?

She had the sudden sense of someone's unseen gaze boring into her. She scanned the shadows but saw nothing. Maybe she should search with the flashlight. Fear licked along her spine at what or *who* she might discover looking back at her. She ran to the back porch and into the house. Her heart thumped, and her scalp crawled. There was no light on in the kitchen, but a soft yellow glow spilled through the hall from the foyer.

She heard Beau call, "It's all clear up here, Nora Lee."

"Down here, too, Sheriff." They seemed to meet on the stairs, and their voices came now in subdued tones.

Deedra forced herself to move toward them, wrinkling her nose at the unfamiliar stench in the air. Nell had told Beau she'd been too afraid to go outside. Maybe the garbage needed taking out. The acrid stench grew stronger with every step and she wondered for a fleeting second what garbage would be doing in this part of the house.

The sight in the foyer froze her.

A woman's thin body sprawled at the bottom of the stairs. Her gunmetal gray hair undone from its bun, her wire-rimmed glasses askew on her narrow nose, and a damp patch of red spread across her blouse and pooled on the hardwood floor.

Deedra didn't have to ask.

She knew Nell was dead.

"Oh, God, Beau. No. No." She spun away, rushing back to the kitchen. She heaved in the sink until her stomach was empty. Using a paper towel, she swiped her mouth with cool water. Beau was on his cell phone speaking with the Butte 911 dispatcher. She switched on the overhead light, needing the shadows and the monsters exposed.

As she spun back to inspect the kitchen, a patch of mint green caught her eye. Identifying the object, she recoiled. Her thundering heart staggered. "Beau!"

Her scream brought him running into the kitchen, gun poised. "What is it?"

She couldn't speak, just point. Spread on the countertop near the stove was a little girl's dress. "It's the same dress I found at Dupont's today."

"Did you touch it?"

"No."

"Don't." He scowled and stepped closer to the dress, his movements careful, protective of the crime scene. "Are you sure it's the same dress?"

"No." She was trembling, but something clicked inside her head. "If it is the one, it'll smell like baby powder."

Gingerly, he leaned over and sniffed. "Maybe it's the dead body, but I can't smell anything else. Certainly not baby powder."

Deedra moved to his side and studied the dress, the smocking at the top, the ribbons at the neck, the tag inside the collar. Her heart slammed into her throat. "Oh, my God, it's not the dress from Dupont's. It's the dress Callie was wearing when she disappeared."

"No." He shook his head. Terror filled his green eyes, terror that she had gone completely insane. But she wasn't crazy. It *was* the dress. She had to make him see it.

"Look, Beau." She pointed. "Look at the tag. Remember, I had her initials embroidered in all of her dresses. In this same gold thread. There they are. *C.C.S.* Callie Cathleen Shanahan."

His face went as white as the ribbons streaming across the mint fabric. The arm holding his gun fell to his side.

"Don't touch it, Beau." Deedra caught his free hand as it reached for this tangible proof that their daughter had survived the accident. Proof that Callie might be alive. "It has to be processed by the lab. That could be our only hope of finding out what happened to her. Of finding her."

Chapter Thirteen

Nora Lee eased around the wall of the archway that led to the foyer. Her gun barrel pointed to the ceiling. Her body was tensed to full alert. "Sheriff?"

"It's okay." Beau jerked free of Deedra's grip, stepped back from the stove and holstered his pistol.

"What's that?" she asked, nodding at Callie's dress. Beau said nothing. She glanced at Deedra who stood to one side, hugging herself.

Beau yanked his Stetson down a notch lower on his forehead, hiding his face. "Our perp has a cruel sense of humor. Go turn on the front porch light. The homicide team will be here momentarily. I want you out there to greet them. Bring them in through the back."

Nora Lee disappeared into the foyer long enough to switch on the light, then passed through the kitchen without a word, respecting that whatever was going on between Beau and Deedra was none of her business.

Once they were alone, Beau slumped against the counter near the sink. There was such agony on his face, Deedra couldn't swallow.

"Callie's dress. Her *actual* dress." His words held pain and sorrow wrenched from deep inside him; he understood now the agony Deedra had felt this afternoon. But this was ten times worse. *Her actual dress.* "And we can't touch it. Oh, God, Dee."

She pressed her fist to her mouth, holding back the tears, seeing in his eyes a feral hope that neither of them dared embrace for fear that this wasn't what it appeared to be.

And yet, how could they not wonder?

Not hope?

She'd struggled so long to accept Callie's death, and now that she had, finally had... The thought that Callie might be alive, might be waiting to be found, that someone had taken care of her these past six months... Someone gentle and kind? Someone cruel and hateful? *Oh, baby mine.*

She began to shake, the tremors deep and as merciless as a riptide tearing at the shores of her sanity. "Is...is it possible? Is Callie...?"

"No." His gaze narrowed on Callie's dress, and he shook his head hard, as if trying to deny the evidence before him. As if he felt the basic beliefs of his life crumbling, all of his truths dissolving into lies. "No. Oh, God, I don't know. If we allow ourselves to believe she is, then discover this is a heartless hoax—could you survive losing her again? I don't think I could."

She swallowed, shoving down the knot that seemed lodged in her throat. The desperation on his handsome face reached out to her, stanching the flood of emotion that threatened to carry her away to the land of the lost—a cruel, pitiless place she wanted never to visit again.

Beau needed her now as he'd never needed her at the beginning of this, after the accident. Once he'd known she would live, he'd chosen to deal with Callie's loss on his own. Alone. Suffering in silence. Adding to the guilt she already couldn't bear.

He'd put his every emotion into his obsession with bringing down Floyd Mann. But Mann was in custody and his capture had resolved nothing for either of them. Had not answered their questions, had not eased their hearts, had not given them any idea as to Callie's fate.

Had not given them closure.

They would only find that, she realized now, by facing this ordeal together.

Resolve sent slivers of heat through the gathering cold that gripped her body, shoving the chill into retreat. The tremors lost momentum, then eased and slowed.

She couldn't look away from her hurting husband. It was as though she were seeing him for the first time. The true Beau. She smoothed her hand down his cheek, felt the pulse jumping at his temple, sensed the tension in his jaw. She deepened her touch, seeking to reach him as he'd reached her, to let him know that she needed him as much as he needed her and that she wasn't going to run out on him this time no matter how rough things might get.

For a long moment their gazes locked, then she asked again the question that shimmered between them. "What if Callie is alive?"

He groaned and a glossy sheen crossed his eyes. Tears. He hadn't shed a single tear over losing Callie. He wouldn't shed them now, but they were there. On his soul.

"Don't you think I want to believe that, too?" His words were a caress, as soft as a baby's breath, as fierce as a father's love. "That I always wanted to believe it?"

Her knees nearly buckled at the admission. She feathered her fingers over the fine lines around his eyes, his mouth, memorizing this rare vulnerable moment, feeling as if he'd laid open his heart to her. In all the time they'd grieved for their daughter, he'd never allowed her to share his pain.

"Oh, Beau, I know you do." Tears stung her eyes. She felt her own heart opening and felt trust taking a tiny step out of the shadows and into the sunlight.

He moaned, shoved his Stetson onto the counter near the sink, and buried his head in his hands. His shoulders slumped as if he were caving in on himself. She pulled him to her, nestling his head on her chest, hugging him. Hate filled her. For the sniper who'd brought this man to his knees. For that unknown woman who'd slashed through their lives like a grim reaper with a deadly scythe.

Beau lifted away from her, his eyes red rimmed, his breath a whisper on her mouth. His sorrow palpable. "Why? Why would someone do something this...this vicious?"

Deedra frowned. It was a strange question coming from a man who'd seen more than his share of the cruelty one human being could inflict on another.

Voices from outside brought them both jerking toward the back door. Beau straightened away from her, flexed his shoulders and schooled his expression as he shoved his Stetson onto his head. Deedra struggled for composure, but felt too spent for pretense. Nell had been murdered and her killer was tormenting Deedra and Beau. In this house of death, they'd found the possibility of hope, but even that didn't console. It only increased the horror of this living nightmare.

Footsteps pounded up the back stairs. Beau squeezed

her hand one last time. "Soon as Nora Lee and you give statements, I'll have her drive you home. I'm going to stick around and make sure no one screws up, that Callie's dress is handled with the utmost care to preserve whatever DNA or other evidence might be on it."

Deedra wanted to stay with him. With Callie's dress. "Beau, I can't leave you…"

"Please, Dee." His eyes pleaded with her, and she saw just how tenuous was the hold he had on his composure. He couldn't bear falling apart in front of his peers.

She stifled her own need to stay with Callie's dress and kissed his cheek, assuring him that she could get through the next hours if he could. But in fact she felt numb, exhausted, her back throbbing. And tired as she was, she wasn't sure she could or would sleep without Beau holding her. Without holding him.

ALONE IN THE BIG BED, Deedra tossed and turned, avoiding sleep, fearing she'd be tortured with dreams of Callie. Eventually exhaustion overtook her, but she didn't dream of her missing daughter. Instead, no matter how often she jerked awake and fell back to sleep, her nightmares had her running through the woods near the accident site, fleeing from some unknown hunter. The hunter carried a high-powered rifle with a precision scope; over her heart, Deedra wore a bull's eye.

The interpretation seemed obvious: the sniper wanted Deedra out of the way, wanted Beau to herself. But for some reason Deedra didn't feel the sniper's anger directed at her. She was just the vehicle, the means to get to Beau. He was the real target. The focus of the hunter's hatred. The one meant to suffer the ultimate wound. To live his life a broken, grief-stricken man.

Robbed of first Callie, then her.

In the next instant, the faceless hunter caught up with Deedra, lifted the high-powered rifle to her shoulder and drew a bead. The explosion echoed through Deedra's ears. Pain radiated across her chest. At first Deedra thought the hunter's bullet had found its mark. She glanced down. Instead of blood oozing from a wound, the bull's eye over her heart was metamorphosing. The red center and the black and white stripes evolved into two human eyes, one mirroring the other. For a long moment she stared, confused, and then she understood.

An eye for an eye.

She startled awake. Daylight filtered into the room, and she was no longer alone. Beau must have come in sometime in the wee hours of the morning. He'd gotten into bed so quietly, he hadn't awakened her. But she felt his warmth beside her now, felt his hand on her waist and heard his gentle snores.

She glanced at him. He faced her, his head deep on his pillow. Her heart sang at the sight of him, the melody a bit happy, a bit melancholy. His raven hair fell over his forehead, his thick lashes brushed his tanned cheeks, and a black shadow filmed his strong jaw. He looked so vulnerable.

Had there been any truth in her dream? Did the sniper want to destroy Beau emotionally?

She shivered at the terrifying thought, more frightened of it than of taking a bullet square in the chest.

She touched his tousled hair lightly, longing to wake him and bury herself and her fears in his embrace. He would tell her that her dream was just that—a dream.

Not real. But seeing his tranquil expression, she couldn't bring herself to disturb him. Let him enjoy the peace while he could.

She would use the time to reason out why she'd been so positive in her dream that Beau was the focus of the killer's nightmare and that she and Callie were merely pawns in the end game.

She eased out from under his arm, slipped out of bed, showered and dressed. Finding the kitchen empty, she helped herself to coffee and settled at the table. The bay window overlooked the barns and corrals. Ranch hands were busy with morning chores, feeding the animals, cleaning the stalls. One was touching up the paint on this side of the barn.

As she watched him dip the brush into the bucket at his feet, she was blindsided by her last image of Callie. Bouncing feet, the soles of her Mary Janes stained red. She'd been fidgety that day, anxious to go "bye-bye" with Mommy, dancing around in her mint-green dress…. "Oh, God."

Coffee washed down the lump that sprang into her throat. Where was Callie? Who had her? Was she being treated with love and kindness? No, God, no. She couldn't go there. Couldn't fall into that pit of fear for her daughter. Not again. It would destroy her.

She forced the thoughts from her mind, pulled her gaze from the window and realized Pilar had left the morning's mail on the edge of the table. Grasping for any distraction, she gathered the small stack of envelopes and began looking through them. Most were bills or letters for Sean or Beau. One stood out. A sweet-scented, card-size envelope addressed to Beau. With a curlicued *E*. Her breath lodged in her lungs. This was from the person who'd written on the bathroom mirror.

The sniper. Deedra's hand began to tremble. She dropped the envelope, struggling not to rip it open and see if there was any mention of Callie.

"That's probably just what you want me to do, isn't it?" she murmured, scooting her chair back. "Destroy all the evidence you left on this."

She hurried over to a bank of drawers, found a freezer-size zip bag, plopped the unopened envelope inside and then closed the seal. She took several deep breaths, several sips of coffee and paced the length of the kitchen twice. Standing behind her chair, she leaned over and smoothed the edges of the bag, examining the envelope through the clear plastic. There was no postmark. It hadn't been processed through the post office.

It had been brought here. Placed in their mailbox out by the road or carried into the house.

But by whom?

Her nape prickled, a shivery sensation that Freddie would have called someone walking over her grave. She raised her gaze to the window and saw Cassidy Brewer, barrel-racing-rodeo-queen-turned-nurse, astride Sassy, her retired champion Appaloosa. She'd forgotten Cassidy boarded her horse at the ranch.

The pretty blonde was speaking animatedly with Sean. She looked gorgeous. Sun glistened in golden hair that hung loose to her waist. Her cheeks were rosy and her eyes flashed flirtatiously. *She really does belong here,* Deedra thought, jealousy stabbing her already wounded heart.

In that moment Cassidy glanced toward the house as if she sensed Deedra's delving stare. As their gazes met, Deedra realized Cassidy's hand had gone to something at her hip. A holster. The pearl-enameled handle of some kind of silver gun poked from its leather depths. Deedra's mind flashed on the hunter in her nightmare. In the next instant that vision dissolved into another—the hunter catching up with her, drawing a bead, the high-powered rifle finding its mark.

An eye for an eye.

"What are you scowling at?" Beau had come on her so quietly she hadn't heard his approach.

She clapped her hand over her lurching heart. "You startled me."

"I'm sorry." Beau hugged her from behind, rocking her gently from side to side and stared out the window. "We're both jumpy."

"Did they find anything on Callie's dress?"

"Not yet, Dee. It's too soon. But they did have the analysis of your pills." His hold on her tightened and his voice softened. "They found arsenic—rat poison— in two of them."

She sucked in a hard breath. It was not unexpected, but still shattering. She shuddered and leaned back into him, glad for his warmth and his strength. The golden-haired nurse was still framed in the window pane. Still staring at her with what looked like pure envy.

Deedra's blood chilled. Had Cassidy tampered with her pills? Was *she* the unknown hunter?

Did she know what had happened to Callie?

Sean had mounted his gray stallion. He signaled to Cassidy, and they trotted off side by side. Deedra asked, "Where are they going?"

"Probably out to check the progress on the hunting cabin repairs. Sean said something about it yesterday."

"Oh?" Why would Sean ask Cassidy to accompany him to look at cabin repairs? Sean's words to Beau echoed in her mind. *You shoulda hooked up with Cassidy. She's as easy on the eyes as they come and she'd give you some big, scrappin' sons to carry on the Shanahan name.* Was he planning on using this opportunity to try to convince the blond beauty to set her cap for Beau?

Or would Sean discover she already had?

She drew a shuddery breath. "Beau, I overheard what Sean said to you the other night about Cassidy. Is there a chance that she's secretly or otherwise in love with you?"

Unexpectedly Beau laughed, then nuzzled her neck. "Mmmm, are you jealous?"

More than he would ever know. She pivoted in his arms. "I'm asking if she has motive to want me dead?"

He peered down at her, his eyes weary but gentle. "Since she was twelve years old, Cassidy has had eyes for no one but Sean. Somehow at that tender age, she extracted a promise from him that he'd marry her when she grew up. But when she grew up, he'd been married twice already and had given up on love. He never took her seriously. Thinks he's too old for her now. But I think Cassidy has made up her mind to land him this time by hook or by crook."

"But he suggested *you* go after her."

"Why would I go after her? I have you." Beau nibbled her neck. "And you must have stopped listening at that point or you'd have heard me tell him to open his eyes and stop fighting the inevitable. If he wants big scrappin' sons to carry on the Shanahan name, then he should father them."

She smiled, relieved and warmed by his response to Sean. "As stubborn as your uncle is, Cassidy will need a hook *and* a crook to rope him in."

"Yeah, well, Sean has no one to blame but himself for that."

Deedra laid her head against Beau's chest, grateful that Cassidy wasn't a threat, but wondering who was. "I guess this means Cassidy didn't leave this."

She plucked the zip bag off the table and handed it to Beau.

"I found it in the pile of mail Pilar left on the table for you and Sean this morning."

Beau released her and took the zip bag between his thumb and index finger. "How'd it get into this?"

"I put it there."

"Good thinking." His gaze had narrowed on the envelope, a hard scowl creasing his forehead.

He'd shaved, she noticed, and cut himself. A tiny nick near his jaw. It wasn't bleeding, but she imagined it had stung something awful. She glanced at the scabs on her palms, recalling skinning them on the pavement where Freddie had died. There had been too much pain these past few days. Too much heartache. But that vile envelope likely held more. "I did touch one corner, Beau, but that's all."

"Couldn't be helped." Agitation was deepening the lines between his eyebrows, tightening his mouth. Beau subscribed to the belief that a man controlled his own destiny. But he'd been robbed of that God-given right the day his daughter disappeared. She ached to ease Beau's anguish, to kiss away his hurt, but what pained him couldn't be healed with kisses or with loving caresses, no matter how heartfelt and well meant. What he needed was some light at the end of this tunnel.

Deedra had none to offer. As anxious as she felt to read this letter, she also feared its contents, feared the news of Callie would be bad.

Beau held the bag to his nose, sniffed and made a face.

"Yeah," Deedra confirmed, wrinkling her own nose. "It reeks of cheap perfume. And there's no postmark. Someone either placed it on the table with the other letters or put it into the mailbox out by the road."

"What did Pilar say about it? Stinking as it does, she would have noticed it while she was separating out the junk mail and magazines. If she didn't, then we know someone came into the house and put it here for us to find."

"I haven't seen Pilar since I came downstairs. She said something last night about today being grocery day. Maybe she's gone to town already."

He glared at the zip bag. His hand shook slightly, a sign that he gripped his emotions as tightly as he'd rein in a runaway horse.

Her own restraint felt near snapping. Not knowing what the note said stirred up her fertile imagination in one awful scenario after the other until she thought she'd scream. Maybe not knowing was worse. "Shouldn't we get it to the forensics lab?"

"This isn't one of her stupid mash notes," he ground out between clenched teeth. "Whatever motivated that 'lovers' ruse ended last night with her leaving Callie's dress for us to find."

"I realize that. Believe me, it was all I could do not to rip it open when I found it."

"I'm surprised you didn't." He touched her hair with gentle fingers, traced her mouth with his thumb. "Get the letter opener."

Deedra froze. Dread and anticipation tangled inside her. "But what if we destroy delicate evidence?"

"I'll be careful, but we're not waiting to find out if

there's something in this note that will lead us to—''
The words choked off and his face darkened.

Why had she even considered they could delay?
Time could be running out, the window of opportunity
slamming shut.

She rushed to the office and collected the letter
opener. Beau tugged on latex gloves. A second zip bag
lay on the table. Holding the envelope partially in and
partially out of the plastic sheath, he sliced the sharp
tip of the opener into the top of the envelope and ran
its razor edge to the other side. He pulled the letter free
with his finger and thumb, gingerly unfolded it, slipped
it into the second zip bag and worked the seal.

Deedra felt light-headed, her heart racing at a diz-
zying pace. She hugged herself, bumping her upper
arm against Beau's, needing that connection no matter
how small—the reassurance that they'd face whatever
they had to together. They leaned over the table and
began reading the note.

Chapter Fourteen

Did you like my little surprise last night? Did it leave you "green" around the gills? I regret not being able to share that moment with you. But I'm sure you understand why I dared not stick around the Widow Carter's until you arrived.

I know the agony of losing a child, but I can only imagine how it felt to discover your precious Callie didn't die six months ago. She didn't toddle off into the woods to succumb to the wild beasties.

And now, you must be aching to know what did become of her....

Does she have a new mommy and daddy?

Is she hidden in plain sight?

Or maybe...she's dead.

Eeeney, meeney, miney, moe.

What happened to Callie?

You'll never know.

Deedra gasped, her hand landing on her chest. She'd thought she'd braced herself for whatever cruelty might be in the letter, but an arrow of pain tore straight through her heart.

"Definitely no mash note. This reeks of hate." Beau's voice was so cold it chilled her. "God, I need some coffee."

He strode to the coffeemaker. He was walking without his cane this morning, with only a slight hitch in his step. She gathered her cup from the table and joined him, getting a refill. Figuring it was time to pitch her new theory. "Beau, what if we've been wrong all this time? What if 'wanting you' isn't what motivates her?"

He refilled her cup first, then filled his own, added two lumps of sugar and stirred with a clanking noise. "Then why target me and mine?"

"Well, this will probably sound strange, but…" She told him about the recurring dream, about her sense that the hunter hated not her but Beau. "It strikes me that there is so much hate around us. Including the hateful act of taking a child from her mother and father."

He considered this. "Well, love and hate *are* opposite sides of the same coin. And she's definitely not using the normal modus operandi of an erotomaniac. The earlier mash notes hinted that she thought she and I were having an affair, though I have no idea who she is. But now that I think about it, if she were a true erotomaniac she'd have killed you and Callie at the accident site. Made sure you were both dead before leaving. She wouldn't have taken our child."

Deedra nodded. "An erotomaniac wouldn't be playing this cat-and-mouse game she's playing with us now, either."

He sipped from his cup. "If we're going to find out the truth about our daughter, we have to figure out why this unsub snatched Callie." His dark eyebrows twitched, and he ran his hand through his hair. He looked dead on his feet. Exhausted and emotionally on the edge. "Figure out why she's trying to kill you."

Deedra felt certain she knew why. Maybe not the specifics, but the general motivation. She could have just told him, but she needed him to see it for himself, to believe as she now believed. "Ask yourself what she's getting out of this? What she's done to *your* life? What has she gained by taking Callie? What will she gain by killing me?"

He didn't answer for a long moment, then he blew out a loud breath. "Losing Callie is like having part of my heart torn from my chest. Your running off, not knowing where you were, stole my will to live, to go on."

Guilt swept through Deedra, and she touched his cheek. "I'm so sorry."

He kissed her hand. "Your death would wipe me out, Dee."

Her heart ached at this admission, but she forced herself to continue, "She brought you to your knees. But you didn't stay there. So, now that I'm back, she's pulling out all the stops, tormenting you as only she can…by using Callie, by destroying me emotionally before killing me."

Light dawned in his eyes. "Revenge."

"Exactly."

The light fled as quickly as it had come. "Yeah, revenge, but damn it to hell, for what? What did I do to her that would make her want to annihilate my life?" He went back to the table and she hurried after him. The note lay where they'd left it.

Deedra couldn't look at it without getting shivers. She forced herself to look at it, anyway. "Maybe there's some clue in this vile message. Something that will give us a place to start looking. Something besides scientific evidence.''

"Tell me where." Desperation ruled his face. He jerked his hand through his hair, his gaze seeming so wild she doubted he could see the actual words on the page.

But her gaze snagged on a line near the bottom of the note, and her heart leaped. Could it be? Was she crazy to even consider it? No. No. At this point, they *had* to look into every possibility. "Beau, remember when I told you I'd run into a pregnant teenager and a couple adopting their first child?''

"Ah, babe, don't go there." His brows dipped together. The fear that she would desert him shone from his eyes. She understood he didn't fear her leaving physically, but emotionally, mentally.

She gripped his hand, reassuringly. "Beau, I'm not going off the deep end. It's that I didn't get the chance to tell you where I ran into them. There's a new lawyer in town. She specializes in adoptions. She even gave me her card.''

"What makes you think she'd have anything to do with Callie?''

"That line." She pointed to the letter, to the words that had made her heart leap: "Does she have a new mommy and daddy?''

"I know it's a long shot, but we can't afford not to check out every possibility. Can we?''

He groaned, but there seemed a little less pain in his eyes. As though he'd caught a glint of that light he sought. "How often have you heard me say that my least favorite part of police work is checking out leads?''

"About as often as you've said it's also the most essential part."

"Yeah." He gave a wry smile. "Because no matter how small or flaky sounding, you never know which lead will be *the* lead. So, tell me how you came to visit this lawyer's office."

She recounted her reason for going into the attorney's and her encounters therein.

He drank his coffee, listening, but she could tell he was unconvinced about something in her story. He scratched his jaw and moved his mug across the table. "You know, darling, it's not against the law to arrange private adoptions."

"I know that." Deedra finished her own coffee. "I guess you need to see her offices and *her* to understand why I doubt T. R. Rudway's legitimacy."

He gathered the zip bags. "Let's get these to the lab, I want a copy of this letter."

Deedra placed their coffee cups in the sink. "And the lawyer?"

"We'll pay her a visit on the way back."

ON THE DRIVE BACK Deedra held the copy of the killer's letter spread on her lap. She couldn't stop looking at the line: "Does she have a new mommy and daddy?" Her stomach, empty of all but coffee, ached. "How are you planning to approach the lawyer? We don't have an appointment. She might have clients there."

"I hope she does." A nerve jumped in his jaw. "I like catching suspects off guard. Gives me a better read on them."

"Are you just going to ask her outright, then,

whether or not she handled the adoption of our daughter?''

He shook his head. ''That isn't likely to get us the results we're after. She could tell us to go to hell. Like I said, we don't know that she's doing anything wrong.''

''Then what are we going to do?''

''You said she offered us her services?''

Deedra frowned and said a cautious, ''Yes, but I wasn't sure which services she meant.''

He glanced toward her. They were just crossing the bridge into town. ''She knew you overheard the couple who was there talking about their adoption, and she told you that she frequents Granny Jo's diner—which means she knows all there is to know about us. I'd say it's a safe assumption that she was offering you her adoption services.''

Butterflies collided in Deedra's stomach. She hadn't ever wanted to consider adoption. Until she'd heard the expectant bliss in the voices of that couple yesterday. But she wouldn't consider it now, not knowing how Sean felt about Shanahan heirs. ''Okay. So, we're going to see her as potential clients.''

''She already knows our story. She'll think we're on the up-and-up. It's the simplest way to find out how she handles adoptions without putting her on the defensive.''

Deedra worried the edge of the copied letter until she'd dog-eared one corner. Could she pull this off convincingly? Granted, she'd participated in hundreds of cons, could probably get a job in Hollywood given her acting skills, but this wasn't play-acting. This was her life. ''I'm not sure she'll consider me fit mother material if she's heard about the Dupont's Department

Store incident, and I'm sure the crowd at Granny Jo's dished out every stinking detail of it.''

"Plus a few made-up ones." Beau patted her hand. "Don't you bring it up. If it's an issue, let her mention it."

"Okay." She folded the note and shoved it into her purse, grappling with her nerves, schooling herself to calm down. But with Callie hopefully at the end of this treasure hunt, Deedra didn't know how to stay calm, cool or collected.

Beau parked in front of T. R. Rudway's law firm, but made no attempt to exit the car. He stared at the building. "Did I ever tell you Rowdy Fortenski hung his shingle here the same year I learned to ride my first pony?"

"No."

"He was my father's lawyer until my parents passed away, and Sean and I inherited him."

"I knew he handled the ranch's legal business until he became too ill to work. How is he?"

"The cancer finally finished him while you were…away. I didn't realize Barb had sold his practice already."

"Well, you'll see soon enough that T.R. didn't purchase it for the local clientele."

He pulled the key from the ignition. "Let's go."

She caught his forearm, a sudden thought dashing the hope she'd nurtured since she'd read the killer's letter a couple of hours ago. "Maybe I'm wrong about T.R. If she handled some bogus adoption of Callie for the killer, then it couldn't have been done here. She's only had this office for two months."

He thought a few seconds, then said, "Or just maybe the woman who took Callie kept her the first four months, then saw an opportunity to pawn her off on someone who wouldn't realize she was our missing daughter. And maybe Ms. Rudway coming to town presented Callie's abductor with both opportunity *and* means.''

''But most everyone in Montana would recognize Callie after the campaign we mounted to find her.''

''Hell, they could have cut her hair short, dressed her like a boy. No one would think she was Callie then. But the older Callie gets, the greater the risk someone in Montana *will* realize she's not whoever her abductor claims she is.''

''Wouldn't possible recognition make adopting her that much harder?''

He considered this, absently touching the nick on his chin. ''Didn't you say the couple you ran into yesterday were from the Deep South and that you wondered whether or not the majority of Ms. Rudway's clients might be from out of state?''

''I guess that would make it less likely that her clients would have seen anything local about Callie being missing. Even with national press coverage, the sad fact is that few abducted children are ever recovered.''

Beau leaned in and kissed her lightly on the lips. ''Can you do this?''

She'd mastered the shell game years ago. The only difference this time was the prize. Callie. That also meant the stakes were higher than for any scam she'd ever run. Her mouth went dry. ''I'm ready.''

''Then let's go see what Ms. Rudway has done with Rowdy's old suites.''

Beau whistled under his breath the moment they stepped into the expensive outer office.

Deedra nodded, speaking in low tones. "Pretty opulent for Buffalo Falls, huh?"

He whispered, "I definitely opted for the bottom of the legal food chain."

She grinned at that. As half owner of the Shanahan spread, he need not have gone to work outside the ranch. But being a full-time cowboy had never fulfilled Beau. He craved the adrenaline rush of brushing up against danger. It was one of the few things they'd always had in common.

No wonder their marriage hadn't been able to sustain a devastating blow. You couldn't build a lifelong relationship on thrills alone. There needed to be substance, too. And trust.

"Looks like her receptionist is on a break," Beau said.

"I'm not sure she has a receptionist." Deedra stepped toward the desk, seeing it was as devoid of work as it had been yesterday. "Don't lawyers require law clerks? Secretaries? At least a personal assistant?"

"Depends—"

T. R. Rudway's door jerked open and the shapely brunette appeared, dressed in a suit of ecru as subtle and as costly as the dove-gray she'd worn the day before. She startled. Obviously she'd expected to be alone, and from the red quickly painting her cheeks it appeared they'd caught her doing something she shouldn't have been doing. Her glance skimmed over Deedra, whom she seemed not to recognize with her hair returned to its normal hue, and snagged on Beau. He had tugged off his Stetson, leaving his hair mussed in an appealing way. He held the hat in both hands like some bashful cowboy. She could see the ploy disarmed the lawyer.

Even *her* heart beat faster.

Give him a woman to charm, and Beau Shanahan was in his element.

He claimed Deedra's insusceptibility to that charm had been what he'd found most attractive about her during their courtship. She liked reminding him that he'd seemed a lot more attracted to her womanly assets than her ability to see through his line of bull.

Beau extended a hand and introduced himself. "Sheriff Beau Shanahan, ma'am. Welcome to Buffalo Falls."

The lawyer clasped her hands together, ignoring his proffered one.

He withdrew it, gripping the brim of his hat again. "If I hadn't known where Rowdy Fortenski's law offices were, I'd have thought I'd stepped through the portals of the *Twilight Zone* when I walked inside here. You sure have spent a pretty penny fixin' this place up."

"Mr. Fortenski's style didn't suit mine." T.R. lifted her chin, her expression tight. "Sheriff, have I broken some local law or are you here selling tickets to the policeman's ball?"

"No tickets. But you ought to know whether or not you've broken any laws."

"None." She assured him, her cheeks reddening again.

"You gave my wife your card yesterday."

"Yes, I did." She shifted toward Deedra. "Nice to see you again, Mrs. Shanahan. You've changed your hair. It becomes you."

Deedra acknowledged the greeting with a nod, not trusting herself to speak. Her stomach clenched with nerves.

The lawyer glanced back at Beau. She brought her arms to her sides, apparently trying to control her nervous hands. She caught hold of the hem of her jacket as if needing to hang on to something. "What may I do for you?"

Beau tilted his head to one side, another of his disarming tactics, but Deedra knew he was taking in the lawyer's unsteady nerves. He didn't miss much. Their presence definitely had her rattled. "Yesterday you offered my wife your services, and we've come to find out exactly what that involves."

Her eyes went cautious. "I assume you're speaking of adoption?"

"Yes, sorry I didn't make that clear," Beau said, grinning so widely his teeth showed.

T.R.'s nostrils flared as she blew out a huge breath. She released the hem of her suit jacket, seeming relieved, on steadier ground. Back in control.

What, Deedra wondered, did that mean?

T.R. glanced at her watch. "I'm expecting clients on the hour. Perhaps you'd like to make an appointment for another day?"

"That's twenty minutes from now," Beau said, not about to be put off. "Can't you spare us any time now?"

"I'm sorry, no. I have to prepare some papers for them." She moved behind the receptionist desk, withdrew a leather-bound book from the top drawer and flipped it open. "I have an opening tomorrow around three if that would—"

"No." Deedra had suffered all the deploying tactics she could stand. She wasn't waiting another day and going through this hell again. "Perhaps you can tell us, then, whether you handle adoptions of children over two years old?''

T.R. blanched as if Deedra had stroked a raw nerve. "How did you find out?''

Chapter Fifteen

Deedra's heart nearly dropped to her toes. "Where is she?"

T.R. reared back as Deedra advanced on her. "She, who?"

"Callie!" Deedra screamed and grasped her arm. "Who did you give my baby to?"

"What are you talking about?" T.R. shook free and rubbed her arm. "Are you crazy?"

"Callie is our missing daughter," Beau said, his soft tone somehow louder in the subdued room than his wife's scream. "Did you arrange an adoption for her?"

T.R.'s hands went to her mouth. "What? No, God, no. I thought you meant—" She broke off, her face flaming, her eyes blinking.

Deedra could almost hear the cogs wheeling in the attorney's pretty head, retracting as she tried coming up with a spin that would undo the damaging words she'd sputtered. It didn't matter to Deedra. T.R.'s shock and honest dismay said it all. She hadn't had anything to do with Callie's disappearance. Deedra bumped back against the wall, her bones turning to melted wax.

Beau, however, advanced on the lawyer, his eyes narrowed like searchlight beams delving into the darkness for clues. The boyish cowboy was gone, the detective stood before them. "What did you think I meant, Ms. Rudway?"

"Nothing, I...I didn't understand the question."

"Don't go there."

"Get out." T.R. was breathing hard. She held the appointment book clasped to her heaving chest, her face as white as its leather cover. "I don't have to answer your questions."

"Like hell you don't. Some lunatic kidnapped our daughter six months ago and has let us think she was dead all this time. She's been trying to kill Deedra and has silenced two other people who could have identified her. So, you see, if you know something and you aren't willing to tell us, then you can cool your heels in my jail for a couple of days while I have your license looked into and go over your whole practice with a fine-tooth comb."

"You can't do that. I'll slap you with a harassment suit."

"Oh, I can and I will. And you can haul me into court, but somehow, I don't think you want to go to court, do you?"

She swallowed hard several times, then sank into the receptionist's chair. "I don't know anything about your missing daughter. I swear I don't. I only handle the adoption of newborns. And then only with the consent of both birth parents. I don't want any unhappy clients on either side of any adoption. Not again."

His eyebrows arched. "Not...again?"

"I thought you knew." She swung wildly toward Deedra. "You said you knew."

"Spill it." Beau's voice was harsh.

She huffed out a long breath. "Let's just say I had

a problem in the past. One time only. I made the mistake of not getting the birth father to sign off on an adoption. When the birth mother brought the boy to me he was almost three. She said his father had run out on her when he found out she was pregnant. That she hadn't seen him since. I found a wonderful couple for the little boy. The week the adoption was to be finalized the birth father showed up. Turned out he had never been told about the child and he very much wanted his son. He took us all to court. My clients sued me, too. I paid for that mistake and will never repeat it, but it ruined my reputation. I had to start over. Reinvent myself. New name. New town. New policies."

"Then why the hell do you look so guilty I'm thinking I should get a judge and a subpoena down here to give me access to your files?"

Tears filled her eyes, and her haughty demeanor crumbled. "I've sunk my last dollar into remodeling this place. I've established new contacts, new clients, a sterling new reputation. Word of mouth, gossip, it can make me or break me. I can't afford to pull up stakes and move again."

Beau fell silent, studying the attorney, taking her measure, deciding whether or not to believe her. But he took nothing at face value. T. R. Rudway wasn't off the hook yet. "Don't think I won't check this out."

"Please do." Trembling like leaves in the aftermath of a violent gust, she gave him her former name and the names and numbers of contacts. "But if you do, Sheriff, please, I'm begging you not to make it public knowledge. No one knows better than you and Mrs. Shanahan how brutal the gossip mill in this town can be. I'm just establishing myself, making friends, really feeling as if I've come home."

Beau rolled his eyes. "Ah, come on. I didn't just fall off a cabbage truck. You're about as country as a New York City cab."

T.R. waved her hand around the room, indicating the decor, then her own designer suit. "Forget all this. It's for the benefit of my clientele. At heart, I'm a small-town Montana girl, more comfortable in my blue jeans on a horse than in this suit driving that leased Lexus out front. Please, don't make me dig up the roots I've planted."

Deedra felt like the one who'd had the roots of hope yanked from her heart. Disappointment pressed down on her like a black cloud covering the sun. But nothing covered the sun as she and Beau stepped outside. Glaring light dug into her eyes and seared her skin. "I think T.R. is telling the truth."

Beau's response didn't surprise her. "She did sound sincere. But then, she's slick. Selling winning arguments is her stock in trade. Give me facts over arguments any day. I'm not taking her word for anything. I just wish I had cause. I'd slap her with a search warrant so fast..."

"And I think we should look elsewhere."

"We'll look everywhere. But first I'm going to the precinct. I want to make a few phone calls and start the ball rolling on that background check."

"Okay." Deedra felt certain it was a waste of time, but when he was this determined, she knew to get out of his way and let him roll. Besides, he'd feel better with that loose end tied into a neat package.

They entered the precinct to find Luanne alone. She sat behind the check-in counter, her wire-rimmed glasses shoved to the top of her head as she scanned a

Rolling Stone magazine. She slapped the cover shut and pulled her glasses onto the bridge of her nose.

"Afternoon, Luanne," Beau said striding toward her. "Has the lab called?"

"No, but you have a few messages." She gathered some pink slips stacked near the phone. "Dr. Warren called twice trying to catch you. She wants an appointment, but I wasn't sure when you'd be free. She'd like you to call her."

Luanne glanced sideways at Deedra as if she knew the psychologist's calls were about her. Deedra's neck warmed.

Shaking his head, Beau accepted his messages and scanned through them. He came back to Deedra and squeezed her hand. "I won't be long. You'll be okay?"

"Uh-huh."

Beau retreated to his office, shutting the door.

Deedra felt Luanne's gaze. She couldn't blame the woman for feeling leery around her after yesterday. She'd terrified Luanne's child. Deedra's behavior could have traumatized Jess. She felt awful about that. She strode to the counter and smiled amiably at Luanne. "I'm sorry about scaring your little girl yesterday. I hope Jess didn't suffer any nightmares."

Luanne seemed surprised at the apology, as if she didn't come from a world where people acknowledged bad behavior. Her cheeks reddened and a wobbly smile tugged at her mouth. "Jess is fine. As Mama would say, she comes from strong stock."

"I'm relieved." And she was. She hated that she might have upset a child. She couldn't bear thinking of the trauma Callie must have suffered from the accident and... Deedra stopped herself, scrabbling for a distraction.

Luanne tugged on her dark curls, and Deedra noticed how pale her skin was, like clear porcelain. The type of skin usually found on natural strawberry blondes. Even her eyes, a pure aqua with golden flecks in the irises seemed more appropriate to someone with fair hair. Had she dyed her hair brown for some reason?

Luanne settled on a lock of hair, catching it with a finger, twisting it. "Ms. Shanahan, what do you think of Dr. Warren?"

The question caught Deedra off guard. "I beg your pardon?"

She twisted the curl tighter, making her finger whiter, and she spoke without taking a breath, spewing thoughts and words in a breathless burst. "Well, I'm going to her for grief counseling for the loss of my best friend, and I know you went to her, too, but after the way you sort of fell apart yesterday, thinking Jess was Callie and all, I just wondered if you felt she was helping you to get better?"

Deedra blinked, taken aback. She didn't know whether to be amused or defensive. She decided on cautious. "I'm no longer seeing Dr. Warren."

"Really?" Luanne's eyes widened. "Why not?"

Okay, edit the earlier thought. Luanne was either extremely guileless or downright snoopy. "I'd rather not go into that."

She sighed so hard Deedra realized it was neither lack of guile nor nosiness. But something personal. "Luanne, do you feel she's helping you?"

"See, that's just it, you know?" Luanne grimaced. "Sometimes I come away from my sessions with her more angry than before I went. I know anger is one of the steps of grief, but shouldn't it start to…what's that big word? Dis-a-something. Oh, yeah—dissipate at some point?''

Deedra stepped back, not sure what to say. She was hardly the one to talk to about dissipating anger, since she was full of rage at the moment. She decided the best tactic would be to take the high road but, all good intentions aside, she couldn't help adding a dash of honesty. "I can't speak for you and I wouldn't presume to question Dr. Warren's treatment for another patient, but her counseling hasn't changed my situation for the better."

Luanne stopped twisting her hair. "Oh, then maybe I *should* see someone else."

"Ah, look, that's up to you."

"Yeah, I know, and changing therapists would mean driving all the way to Butte once a week. What with the price of gas these days, well, it would just be more than I could afford. Besides, my insurance is already paying for Dr. Warren." A look of resignation controlled her pale, oval face. "And she is the one who does psychological evaluations for the Buffalo Falls P.D., which saves me having to repeat all my secrets to someone else, someone new, you know?"

"I didn't know Dr. Warren handled the psychological evaluations for the B.F.P.D. How long has that been the case?"

"Oh, she just started. Just finished them, I should say. We've all been to her now, Nora Lee, Heck, Sheriff Shanahan and me."

Beau had been analyzed by Dr. Warren? He hadn't mentioned it, but then he might not, since it was work related and required by city council. She could only imagine how uncomfortable he had been being dissected by that woman. Dr. Warren hadn't been a fan of his during Deedra's sessions, and Deedra had since begun to suspect the psychologist disliked men.

Luanne intruded on her musings. "She really wants a baby, you know?"

"Who?"

"Dr. Warren. Who else are we talking about?"

"I didn't think she was married."

"You don't need to be married to have a baby these days."

"Who is she dating?"

"Local gossip says no one." Luanne leaned closer and lowered her voice. "I heard someone at Granny Jo's say that no man would want to bed a…a ball-buster like her."

Deedra shook her head. "There are always sperm banks."

"Yeah, but then, she's been getting cozy with that new lawyer, Ms. Rudway. Maybe she's gonna buy herself a kid."

Deedra felt the color drain from her face. Her thoughts and suspicions ran back to the lawyer. Had Beau been right about T. R. Rudway being a slick liar? Had Deedra totally misread her? And what about the shrink? Deedra had poured out her heartache over losing Callie to that woman. About Beau's emotional distancing. Revealed some of her deepest fears. Would Dr. Warren use those secrets against her?

Had either woman had something to do with Callie's disappearance? Or was she grasping at any possibility?

"I really wish you'd help me figure it out." Luanne cut into her musing.

"Figure what out?" Deedra had gotten lost in her thoughts and had no clue what Luanne meant.

"Whether or not I should keep seeing Dr. Warren."

"You know, I'm not the only patient of hers you could consult for an opinion on this. Have you asked Nora Lee or Heck what they think of her?"

"Uh-uh. I didn't even start to wonder about whether or not she was helping me until you…well, until yesterday."

"I'm sorry if I caused you to distrust your therapist. Trust is vital to such a relationship."

"It's just…I'm still so pissed off that my friend was killed."

Shock riveted Deedra. "Your best friend was murdered?"

"No. Yes. Well, some I know say that. But I'm not sure what I believe."

"I'm sorry for your loss, Luanne. I know how it hurts to lose someone you love."

"Yeah, I guess you do." Luanne caught her hair again. "Thanks for talking to me about this. But please don't tell anyone I was asking. I wouldn't want it to get back to Dr. Warren."

"I won't tell a soul."

Luanne rolled her magazine lengthwise and stuffed it into a tote bag on the floor. A pink teddy bear stuck up from the bag, reminding Deedra of Callie's bunny, reminding her that she still didn't know where it was. Could it have been held as evidence? If so, it would be stored here, somewhere. "Say, Luanne, I know you were working for Sheriff DeMarco at the time of my accident."

"Yes, I was."

"Do you know where the records of my case might be?"

Behind her glasses, her aqua eyes were curious. "Open-case files are kept in the sheriff's office."

"What about cold-case files?"

"Sheriff DeMarco stored all those in the basement. In boxes. I suppose your case could be there. I mean, they never did figure out who cut your brake line, right?"

"Right." Deedra forced herself to keep her tone even. "Do you think we could have a look?"

Luanne gave an uncertain glance at Beau's closed door, then studied Deedra. "Why? What are you looking for?"

"I don't remember the accident. I've been wondering if seeing the crime-scene photographs again might jar some memories loose. Something that might give us a lead to finding out who's trying to kill me."

Uncertainty seemed to drain from Luanne to be replaced by sympathy. "Well, sure. Why not? But I can't go with you. It's nearly time for me to head home and give Mama some relief. Jess just plumb wears her ragged some days."

"It's nice that your mother can watch her for you."

"Oh, Jess is just one of the kiddies she watches. She and my aunt run a day care."

Deedra blanched at the mention of a day care, thinking of Nell and the funeral she would be planning as soon as the Butte police released the body for burial. "Is the day care here in Buffalo Falls?"

"No. It's between here and Dillon." She found a ring of keys from her desk and handed them to Deedra. "It's the key with the big *E* painted on it. Your case file should be easy enough to find. The boxes are stacked by the month and year and clearly marked."

Deedra bade her goodbye and then hurried into the back of the building. One hallway led to the holding cells. Another hallway led to the bathrooms, an exit and the basement stairwell.

"DR. WARREN, this is Beau Shanahan. I understand you want to speak to me about something."

"I told you that yesterday. I've been trying to make an appointment, but Luanne doesn't seem to know when you'll be in the office." Her tone made it clear she disapproved of his not keeping regular office hours.

"I've had pressing business." He leaned back in his chair. "What do you need?"

"This is a very delicate matter, and I'd like to speak about it in person."

"I'm here now."

"Unfortunately, I have a patient coming soon and can't leave."

"Then you'd best spill it now."

She hesitated long enough that he thought she might have hung up. "Doctor...?"

"Yes." She blew air down the line. "Someone has been rifling my patient files."

"You've had a break-in?" Beau sat straighter and instinctively reached for a tablet and pencil, ready to take notes.

"Well, not if you mean someone broke a window or the locks or anything."

"Then spell it out."

"The tapes of my sessions with one of my patients are missing."

Beau knew from his time on her couch that Dr. Warren recorded her counseling sessions. He grimaced, stuffing down the memories. Jed Bartley and his fool notions. He watched too many network cop shows. Jed, Buffalo Falls' mayor, had insisted the city council pass-a law requiring Beau's whole damned staff to undergo psychological evaluation. Complete waste. They didn't suffer the kind of burnout stress that warranted concern. "So, no one broke in?"

"No."

He began writing on the tablet. "When did you notice the tapes were missing?"

"The other day. The day your wife went…had the incident at Dupont's."

He ignored the obvious dig at Deedra. "So, you think it was one of your patients who stole the tapes?"

"I think it was you."

"Me?" His hand froze over the note page. "Have you lost your mind? Why would I steal tapes from you? Nothing that went on in our sessions has me losing sleep at night. You're free to report it all to the city council."

"They weren't your taped sessions that were stolen. They were Deedra's."

"What?" The pencil snapped beneath his hold.

"And who else would care what was in them except you?"

Beau could think of someone, and the thought galvanized him. But what the hell would the killer want with those, except to further torment Deedra?

DEEDRA STEPPED WITH CARE down the ancient wooden stairs that led to the basement. This building had been one of the first built in town. Parts of its structure dated back to the years when outlaws roamed free and wild. At the bottom, the stairs ended on a wooden landing. Straight ahead a solid door was marked Janitor. Behind the staircase was another door, marked Evidence. The air-conditioning cooling the main floor hadn't been piped to this area, and heat seemed trapped in the tight space.

She stepped to the second door and inserted the key, thinking what a joke it was to lock a door when the top portion was glass. Obscured glass, but still breakable. Then again, maybe security wasn't an issue, given the few serious crimes that occurred annually in Buffalo Falls.

The door shoved open easily on well-oiled hinges. She switched on the overhead light. The bulb cast a dim glow, doing nearly nothing to eliminate the shadows from the musty space. The room was huge. Eerily quiet. Hot and airless. Sweat trickled down the sides of her face, between her breasts. She left the door wide open.

Tall metal storage shelves, sharp-edged and spindly, stood against all four walls and formed three rows in the center. To her surprise, the shelves were stacked full of storage boxes dating back to the end of the 1800s. Some of the cardboard containers seemed to be deteriorating. Too bad no one had started putting this information on microfiche or into a computer before the oldest of the case files—some indicative of the very early history of Buffalo Falls—were lost forever. She'd have to speak to Beau about it. Surely this would be a better use of Luanne's working hours than magazine reading.

She began searching and found that the oldest files occupied the shelves against the walls. The newer ones would be in the center of the room somewhere. As she moved between the racks, touching this one and that, the shelves creaked and wobbled, making her wonder just how sturdy they were.

Halfway into the second row, she found the box she

sought on a bottom shelf. She squatted and grasped hold of it. Movement in her peripheral vision brought her jerking back. She glanced up and caught sight of a nasty looking spider adding strands to its web. She shuddered and inched away. It was high enough not to worry about it scurrying down to bite her, but where there was one spider, there were likely others.

She shirked off the thought and tugged the box marked "Shanahan" onto the concrete floor, daubing sweat from her forehead. The lid came off, releasing a musty odor. Atop reams of paperwork, the photograph of the accident scene glared up at her. She stared at the image that was seared into her mind. She hadn't forgotten one detail of it. Could have drawn it, point for point, though she was not an artist. Her mouth dried, and sweat pooled in the small of her back.

The Jeep lay against the downed tree. Tipped on its side. Windshield cracked. Child's safety seat empty.

The bunny—all six inches of pink fluff with white satin inside its floppy ears—sprawled alone on the dirt road. Not as if it had flown free during the wreck. As though it had been dropped.

Where was it? She dug to the bottom of the box. No bunny. "It should have been here."

Unless Beau…

A shuffle near the door brought her head up. "Beau?"

No one answered, and she started to stand. "Is someone there?"

She felt a shiver down her spine, as if the spider had somehow stolen inside her clothes and crawled against her skin. She jerked toward the insect. It still hung in its web. She shuddered, feeling shivery all over. She hunkered down again, shoved the lid back on the box and replaced the box on the shelf. A metal creak behind her brought her lurching around.

Too slow. Off balance.

The shelf at her back, loaded with boxes, toppled straight at her.

Chapter Sixteen

A short while later, the sniper stood across the street from the office on Custer. Hugging the shadows. Watching for the next victim. Killing the day care woman had been daring and necessary, but not as much of a high as running down her sleazy son. *That* had been an adrenaline rush. Wiping out lowlifes always was. But face-to-face combat—that could be risky. Mrs. Carter's feisty resistance had made it more so. She'd folded easily enough, though, faced with the pistol. She'd turned into a sorry, pathetic old hag begging for her life. Swearing she wouldn't tell.

She'd been right. She wouldn't be telling anyone anything.

She should have been the last loose thread.

The last obstacle to the main target.

But damn it all, now another nosy Parker threatened. Another squealer that had to be silenced.

Too bad the killing did nothing to lessen or assuage the rage. It only increased the need to make Beau Shanahan pay.

Had he found his precious Deedra yet?

Would she be merely stunned? Critically injured? Crippled? Bleeding internally?

Or had the heavy metal shelf struck a fatal blow?

Whichever, Beau Shanahan would soon know the cost of what he'd done, would soon reap the devastation his thoughtless orders had sown.

Maybe watching him implode will douse these flames of hatred and bring closure for me and my family.

A form appeared in the office window grabbing the killer's full attention. *Ah, there she was.* As per her weekly routine, she'd closed at noon today, but she hadn't gone home. She'd retreated into the private back room. Her workout area.

The woman in question stood spread-legged, lifting miniweights to her chest in repetitive jerks. *Obsessed bitch ought to see a therapist about her compulsion to exercise. Or couldn't she admit to herself that she was as neurotic as some of her patients?*

Hadn't planned on killing her. Not here. Not today. But she'd discovered Deedra's tapes were missing. Had been trying to reach the sheriff. She had to be stopped now, before she recalled who had access to her locked cabinet. But there wasn't time to run home for the silencer, and a normal gunshot in this part of town would draw a crowd. No, she wouldn't die from a bullet. But how?

Watching the muscles flex in the shrink's upper arms, the killer considered the best approach. This was no easy prey. No slack-bodied hag who would fold at the sight of a weapon. No grief-stricken mother distracted by thoughts of her missing child.

She would be leery. On guard. Best to disarm her emotionally. First by this surprise visit. Second by asking her for something she'd need to go after, that would cause her to turn her back. And third by catching her from behind.

Yeah. That was it. Make it look like an accident. Like she'd tripped and fallen into the shaft of her heavy metal workout bench and cracked open her head.

Beau might *think* it was murder. Might even *know* it. But he wouldn't be able to prove it.

Grinning, the killer hurried to the office. The door was unlocked. No one locked their doors in Buffalo Falls. The killer slipped into the empty reception area. The back portion of the building was divided into two rooms. The doctor's office and her exercise space.

The predator listened to its prey, huffing and puffing, working off imagined fat. Imagined cellulite. The killer crept across the reception area. The door swung easily inward. "Dr. Warren, I was hoping to catch you here."

Chapter Seventeen

By the time Beau finished returning phone calls, his gut was in a knot. It hadn't been enough for the evil bitch to steal their daughter. No, she had to take the tapes of Deedra's personal conversations with her psychologist. Had to invade Dee's privacy, violate her most intimate feelings, denigrate her grief. He felt sickened. Infuriated. If the sniper had stood before him at that moment, he would have killed her with his bare hands.

He shoved off from his desk and stalked to the coatrack for his hat, all but choking on impotent rage. *Dee!* Oh, God, how could he tell her? Hell, did he have to tell her? He blew out a hard breath. He'd promised there would be no more secrets between them. And he'd broken too many promises in the past. If he kept it up, even for her own good, they wouldn't survive whatever new hell loomed on the horizon.

Callie. His little girl's image froze his hand on the knob, and the strangling lump in his throat wrenched tighter. He groaned and yanked open the door of his private office. He had to keep moving or the agony of wondering where his little girl was would kill him, would stop his heart dead in his chest.

The booking area was a wasteland of unpeopled desks and deserted workstations. Neither of his deputies had returned, and Luanne seemed to have left for the day. "Deedra?"

She didn't answer. She wasn't impatiently pacing the precinct waiting area. Had she gone out to wait in the car? He couldn't picture her being comfortable on the street, not in this heat, not exposed as that would make her to the prying eyes of curious townsfolk…or to the sniper.

He checked, anyway.

Late-afternoon sun bore down, glaring off windshields and into his eyes. His car still nudged the curb. He had to walk right up to the passenger door to determine no one sat inside. Worry and heat brought moisture to his skin. He scanned the street in both directions, wiping a trickle of sweat from his temple. No sign of her.

No sign of her. The fear he'd lived with the two months after she'd run away seized him, tore through his belly like razor-edged spurs slicing open scabbed-over wounds. Had she run away again? Left him to face this hell alone? No. He'd laid his heart open to her. He'd told her it would kill him if he lost her. He'd seen the aching pain his admission had caused her and had known in that moment that she would never run out on him like that again.

Especially not now. Not when Callie might be alive.

But if she hadn't taken off, then where the hell was she? And why hadn't she let him know where she was going? A horrible thought struck him, and his skin grew cold beneath the staggering sun. Maybe she hadn't been able to tell him. Maybe leaving hadn't been her idea.

Cursing under his breath, he hurried into the precinct and began searching for something—a note, anything—that would give him a clue to her whereabouts. He checked Luanne's desk first. Then Nora Lee's and finally Heck's. Nothing. Damn it.

A noise from the back hall pulled him around. *Oh, God. Of course, she was in the ladies' room.* He slumped against Heck's desk and released a heavy sigh. Fear fell from him like shed weight, and Beau chuckled at himself. *Idiot. Should have checked there first thing.* He crossed to the water dispenser, filled a paper container and drank.

Nora Lee came through the front door. He'd sent her to Butte to find out what the crime scene investigators had turned up at Nell Carter's house. To check on autopsy results. He asked, "Anything we didn't already know?"

She dragged her Stetson from her head, ice-blond hair sticking up in spikes, and wiped at her forehead. Her faded-blue eyes were bright and her cheeks had the rosy glow of someone standing too long in the sun or someone who'd been strenuously exerting herself. "It was like you figured. A forty-five caliber shot to the heart at close range. Apparently, Mrs. Carter put up a struggle, but there was no tissue under her nails. Guess they deduced the struggle from blood spatter, scuff marks on the floor and that overturned lamp. They're still checking her clothing for hair and fibers and latents."

Beau nodded, disappointed, his patience near snapping. He hated biding his time, waiting for answers that would give them something to work with, somewhere to start. Some way to find his daughter. "What about Callie's dress? Have we heard anything on *that* yet?"

"No. I called about it on my way back here. They're still processing it."

"They call this a rush?"

"Believe me, Sheriff, they know what's at stake."

She said the last with so much sympathy, his breath hitched and his response came out gruff. "Yeah, I know."

Heck hustled into the building. He headed straight into the men's room without greeting either of them. Beau could hear the water running, and his mind jerked back to Deedra. She should have been done in the bathroom by now. What was taking her so long? Some complication related to her health problem? Alarm sent him running to the back hall.

Two rest rooms stood at the head of the hall across from each other, the basement stairwell halfway down and an exit door at the end. He thumped the ladies' room door. "Deedra?"

No answer. His pulse kicked a notch higher. "Deedra? Are you okay?"

He banged the door open. The tinny stench of rusty water and aged pipes swept out, but the room—closet-size, only large enough for a sink and toilet—was empty.

Nora Lee came up behind him. "Sheriff, what's wrong."

"Deedra. She was waiting for me with Luanne an hour ago. But when I came out of my office, she was gone."

"You think they went somewhere together?"

"No…" Why would she? Where would she? "I…I don't know."

"You want me to call Luanne?"

Heck came out of the men's room looking relieved

and catching the tail end of their conversation. "I passed Luanne on my way back into town. She looked to be headin' home."

"Was Deedra with her?" Beau asked.

Heck shook his head. "Far as I could see she was alone in her pickup."

"Maybe Ms. Shanahan told Luanne where she was going," Nora Lee said. "I'll phone her and ask."

Before she took a single step, Heck pointed at something behind them. "Hey, who left that open?"

Beau and Nora Lee jerked around. The exit to the alley was always kept shut, locked from the inside. Now it stood slightly ajar.

Nora Lee lifted puzzled blue eyes at Beau. "Would Ms. Shanahan use this exit?"

Beau didn't even want to guess the reason Deedra would have for that. He strove to hide the depth of his distress from his deputies with a shrug. "Why would she?"

Nora Lee shook her head. "I don't know. I'm just asking."

Heck strode past the stairwell to the back exit. He kicked the door wider and peered outside. "Nobody out here 'cept a coupla rats chawing down in the garbage cans."

He came back in and pulled the door tight. The lock engaged with a click.

Heck's face was flushed. "You worried Ms. Shanahan's gone off on—" He broke off, rethinking his callous question. "That maybe she mighta had another...episode like the other day?"

"No," Beau barked the word, chopping it off the way he'd like to chop off his mounting worry.

Heck's neck reddened as if Beau had chopped it instead of his word. He pointed toward the booking area. "I got some reports to finish up."

Beau nodded and stared at his feet, grappling with his disquiet.

"I'll call Luanne," Nora Lee said.

"Okay." He hit the hall switch, dousing the overhead light, but a dim glow of yellow still warmed the end of the corridor near the stairwell. Frowning, he stepped to the landing and glanced down. The light shone from below. The nape of his neck prickled.

"Luanne's not home yet."

Nora Lee's approach startled Beau. He glanced over his shoulder at her. "Did the janitor forget to turn off that light again?"

"He hasn't been here this week." She was frowning. "You think Ms. Shanahan's down there?"

He called down, "Deedra?"

Silence wrapped them, stirring a niggling unease in Beau's belly and along his nerves. In low tones he told Nora Lee to get Heck and cover his back. He drew his gun from his holster and started down. It felt like what he imagined it would feel like to descend into hell: hot…hotter…hottest. Until the air seemed to hold no oxygen.

Boiling in summer, freezing in winter. That could not be good for the papers stored down here, he thought abstractly. If his life ever returned to normal, he would check into correcting that before all of the case files were lost forever.

But first things first.

"Deedra?" His voice echoed back at him, wrapping him with unease. He moved with caution. Each tread creaked beneath his weight. At the bottom of the stairs, he found the janitor's door closed and locked. He drew a lungful of the heavy air. Readied his gun. Schooled his muscles. "Whoever you are, you're cornered. So, come on out."

No response.

He charged the evidence room. The door hung open. Horror ripped into him and he swore. Two of the center shelves had toppled like tipped dominoes against each other and into an end wall. Boxes had dumped, papers flown everywhere as though a minitornado had blown through.

Heck clambered down the stairs, then stopped dead in his tracks at the doorway. "Holy crap. What a frickin' mess. How the blazes did this happen?"

"Unless we had an earthquake I didn't feel, I'd say someone did this on purpose."

"What purpose would that be?" Heck scratched his head. "'Cept to cause us one helluva mess to pick up."

"And who?" Beau caught the keys dangling in the lock and pulled them free. *Deedra?* He jerked back to the wrecked room. His heart thundered. His gut roiled.

Heck said, "Luanne must've given the key to someone. That there is her set."

A low moan issued from somewhere within the pile of rumble. Beau jolted. "Dee! Nora Lee, get Dr. Haynes! Now!"

Fear for his wife broke free. What would Deedra want to see in this room? Her case file? But why? He wanted to tear through the debris, rip away the twisted metal and disgorged boxes, but, terrified he'd hurt her more than she might already be, Beau moved with care. He instructed Heck to do the same.

Slowly, torturously, they cleared a path. Beau kept calling her name, speaking to her, reassuring her that he was coming. Deedra didn't answer. She didn't moan again. Fear tumbled inside him. Then he saw a patch of blue. The blouse she'd been wearing.

Beau grabbed one edge of the first shelf, shouting at Heck. "Help me get this off her!"

They levered it up and away from Deedra. Beau dropped to his knees beside her prone body.

"Geeze." Heck's foot came down hard on the concrete flooring. "Frickin' black widder. It didn't bite Ms. Shanahan, did it?"

Had it? Fear coiled in Beau's belly. He lifted a box from her abdomen. Blood leaked from her forehead, the way it had when she'd been injured in the accident with Callie. Her face was ashen. Her pulse weak. The air was more stagnant here than in the stairwell area. Too little oxygen. And she was too still.

His mind filled with visions of nearly losing her after the Jeep wreck. With the agony he'd felt during those long days and nights pacing the hospital corridors. With all the ugly, unimaginable scenarios he'd conjured of where she was and what might have happened to her during her two-month absence.

This morning Dee had said the killer wanted to bring him to his knees. He'd said the only thing that could do that was losing her.

Beau's heart cried.

BEAU PACED THE CORRIDORS of the hospital, wearing grooves into the same tiles he'd paced six months ago, waiting for word on Dee's condition. Then, and now, the waiting was interminable. Sean and Pilar and even Cassidy had joined him, bringing him coffee, offering reassurances, praying. None of it eased the fear in his gut.

All he knew was that the spider hadn't bitten her and

that she was unconscious. Tests. They were running tests. His life seemed one big mass of tests lately. Results. That's what he needed. Positive results. For Deedra. For Callie. For himself.

"What's taking so long?" Beau asked no one in particular.

Cassidy had been standing to one side, still dressed in her nurse's uniform. "Let me see what I can find out."

She disappeared into the examination room. The next five minutes felt like five hours. Cassidy returned, her expression so gentle Beau's muscles went taut, the flesh on his face tightened, the moisture in his mouth vanished. His breath jammed. So great was his fear, he couldn't speak. Couldn't ask the question.

Sean asked it for him. "Is she going to be okay?"

"She'll be fine. She's a bit dehydrated. Has a slight concussion. Nothing as serious as six months ago. But the doctor wants to keep her overnight for observation."

Doctors always wanted to keep patients overnight. That didn't bother Beau. Deedra's female problems of late had his imagination tripping over worries of internal bleeding, of hemorrhaging. Silently he pleaded for Cassidy to understand without his having to say it. "I lifted a heavy box from her stomach. I…I think it struck her abdomen when it fell."

To his relief Cassidy caught the gist of his fears. She shook her head, her long braid slapping her shoulders. "No internal bleeding. She has some cuts and contusions, one really nasty bruise on the area near her left hipbone. The doctor said something heavy likely struck her there, so I'd guess that's probably where the box impacted. It will be sore for a few days, but nothing permanent, nothing to worry you.''

Nothing to worry him? He'd believe that when he saw her with his own eyes. ''Is she conscious? Can I see her?''

DEEDRA ACHED as if a semi-truck had plowed into her. Her head, her hip. Her everything. Oddly, though, not her back, for once. What the hell had happened? She touched a hand to her forehead, felt a bandage, and it all came back. The scuff of a footstep. The shelves tipping over, boxes falling, all of it landing on her. Beau's voice sifting through the black fog.

She opened her eyes, and he was standing there. Beside the hospital bed. He smiled and his handsome face lit as if from within. The love in his eyes caused her heart to ache with pleasure.

He took her hand and held it over his heart. Her pulse beat in tune with his. He didn't speak, and she knew he needed a few minutes to rein in emotions that he would deny feeling if asked. Emotions he'd only recently shared with her. She gave him the time, reassuring him she would be okay.

''I met Dr. Barzelli,'' she said. ''He'll be performing my surgery in six weeks. He's been reading up on my case and says there's a new procedure for which he thinks I might be a good candidate. He's going to give us brochures to study. But he insists I don't do anything too strenuous between then and now.''

''Like getting yourself buried beneath boxes and storage shelves?'' Beau's voice was gruff, the emotion not quite under control.

He wanted to know why she'd been in the evidence room. But he hadn't asked. Suddenly she didn't want to ask him about Callie's bunny. If he'd taken it home, then she needed to let it be for now. She didn't need to invade that private moment of his grief for their daughter.

She said, "I hoped looking at the accident photos again might jar loose a memory, or that I'd see something in the pictures that would give us some idea of how to find Callie."

"And did it help?" He searched her face as she had searched the photographs, the same hope in his eyes as she'd held in her heart. "Did you remember?"

She pressed her lips together and shook her head, wincing at the pain that ran across her skull. "Ouch."

Sympathy softened his expression. "You have a slight concussion."

"I know. Why don't you get me released from this place and take me home? I need some of your special TLC."

"Sorry, babe. But the doctor wants you to spend the night. They're readying you a room at this very moment."

"No!" Fear rushed through her. "Don't leave me here, Beau. I'm afraid. I won't be safe. Not here."

He lifted her hands and kissed them. "Ah, babe. I'm not going anywhere. I'll be right at your side all night long."

"Really?"

"Really." He kissed her cheek. "In fact, I'll even post a guard outside the room once you're settled. Okay?"

"Okay." She gathered a shuddery breath and sank back on the pillow, her head thumping, her hip achy.

"Dee, I know you're exhausted and hurting, but I

have to know. Did you see who pushed the shelves over on you?''

''No. I heard a scuffing. But then it stopped and I thought I might have imagined it, or that it was a mouse. So, I shoved the box back onto the shelf intending to get out of there. But I wasn't quick enough.''

''It's very likely your being slow kept you from getting injured worse than you were.'' He kissed her hand again.

''It's so frustrating, not being able to do something to find Callie. Did you find out anything new about T. R. Rudway?''

''I made the calls and everything was just the way she said it would be.'' He ran his hand across his hair, mussing it, frowning as if bothered by something.

''What is it?''

''Nothing. Except my gut telling me something about T.R.'s past is as slick as the lady herself.''

''What?''

''I don't know.'' He shrugged. ''It's nothing I can put my finger on...but something seems...too pat.''

She sighed, her frustration sitting in her throat. ''Is there any news on Callie's dress yet?''

''Last I checked they said they'd maybe have something in the morning. They'd better—because this waiting is killing me.''

''It's killing me, too.''

They held hands for a while, joined by love and fear and the thread of hope that they might soon hold their daughter once again.

If only they could find her.

The nurse came and wheeled Deedra to a private room. While they settled her, hooking up an IV to counter the dehydration, Beau called Heck to man the hall outside her room throughout the night.

Once they were alone, Deedra suggested, ''Maybe we should look at her note again. Maybe that will give us something to go on. It's in my purse.''

Nora Lee had brought the bag over from the precinct, and he'd seen the nurse place it in the room's metal closet. He found it and handed it to her. Deedra pulled out the copied note.

Beau sat on the edge of the bed, cradling her against him and read over her shoulder. She shivered at the end, as violently as she had when she'd first read it. But this time something struck her that hadn't before. Maybe it was because her head hurt so badly her concentration had narrowed and shoved out extraneous matter.

An eerie excitement caught her. ''Look, Beau, she says she knows what it feels like to lose a child.''

His gaze zeroed in on the line in question. ''What has that got to do with why she's trying to bring me to my knees?''

''I don't know.'' She twisted around and gazed up at him. ''Were you ever involved in a case where a child lost his or her life?''

''No. God, no. You know how I feel about kids.''

''Did you ever investigate the death of a child? Perhaps proving the prime suspect didn't do it? A case that ended up unsolved?''

''Never.'' He released her and stood, pacing across the room, staring out the window.

Deedra laid her head on the pillow again and shut her eyes, listening to the tumble of thoughts spinning through her brain. Bits and pieces of everything she'd believed and imagined and felt since Callie had disappeared whirled round and round in her mind like colored chips in a kaleidoscope. Suddenly a design fell into place. She levered herself up on her elbows, ignoring the pain that sprang from too many sources. "There was one case, Beau, where a child died. An unborn child."

Beau pivoted toward her. His tanned face went pale and filled with pain, as much from the guilt that he would always feel as from realization.

Her voice rang with reverence, with respect for the dead mother and child, "Merry Sue Mann's unborn baby."

Beau knew she was right, but his eyes darkened, grew pensive, thoughtful. He started shaking his head. "It can't be. Mann is behind bars. He sure as hell isn't doing this to us."

No. He couldn't be. She shifted on the bed, moving gingerly to avoid more pain. "Might he have an accomplice bent on revenge?"

Beau blinked as though she'd struck him. "You mean a family member?"

"Why not?"

"Because Floyd Mann is a loner. He doesn't 'team' well. It's why he bailed out of the white supremacists. Or why they kicked him out. He has no family as far as I could ever discern."

"How about Merry Sue?" She warmed to this new idea, sensing she'd hit on the thing that had been eluding them all this time. "Did she leave behind family members who might want to avenge her death, the death of her unborn child?"

Beau froze, his expression saying it all. He'd never

considered that side of the tragedy, Merry Sue's family's side. "As soon as you're released in the morning, I'll take you home, then I'm heading to Butte to talk to Mann again."

Chapter Eighteen

Floyd Mann. He reminded Deedra of an ogre even more now than he had the first time she'd sat in this room and watched through the two-way mirror as Beau interrogated him. She lowered herself gingerly onto the hard plastic chair, careful of her bruised hip and grateful the sharp-edged metal shelf hadn't stabbed into her belly. Or her neck. Or somewhere else equally vulnerable.

The concussion had pain lingering against her temples and across her skull. She strove to ignore these physical aches and concentrated on the men in the other room.

Just as before, Mann hunched in a metal chair across the table from Beau. Defiance scrunched his curmudgeon face. The swastika tattoos reminded her that this was not a man who'd be easy to handle. Or one who was likely to cooperate. But he had to. He just had to.

Mann laced his fingers together as if he wanted to be sure Beau didn't miss the message K-I-L-L-C-O-P-S etching the flesh above his knuckles. "Walkin' without the cane, I see," he said, a sneer in his gravelly voice. "Too bad the damage inflicted on me won't heal so quick. If ever."

Despite his worst crimes, Deedra felt a pang of empathy for Mann. She knew how it felt to have the most cherished thing in one's life ripped away. Knew that sudden sense of irreplaceable loss. But she felt no pity for how he'd handled his grief. He'd gunned down another man, a father, and devastated another family as he'd been devastated. That kind of vengeance always came back harder on the one exacting it.

As it ought to on the people who had snatched Callie. The ones who were still trying to destroy her and Beau.

Beau's face had turned steely at Mann's barb, but she knew he would always hold himself to blame for the accidental death of Merry Sue and her unborn child. He would always regret a decision he couldn't change, a decision that had changed not only Mann's life but his own. Her own.

Beau leaned on the table separating him from Mann. "What was it you said to me last time I was here? Oh, yeah. You said, 'I ain't the one after you. Not me.'"

Something shifted in Mann's watery blue eyes, and he dropped his gaze and turned his head to the side. But he didn't deny it.

"But you know who is, don't you?"

Mann ignored him.

Beau slapped the table with his palm. Mann's head snapped up, his eyes jumping. Beau growled. "Don't you!"

Mann ran his tongue over his lips. "I got my suspicions."

"Who?"

He laughed, a nasty bark that held no humor but dripped of sarcasm. "What would my tellin' you get me?"

Deedra's heart sank inside her chest. Mann was likely to be convicted as a cop killer and receive life in prison or the death penalty. There would be no deals for him. No lighter sentence. Nothing Beau could barter that Mann would care about enough to oblige him.

Beau arched an eyebrow. ''Tell me about Merry Sue's family.''

Mann's eyes widened in amazement. Beau had landed on the truth. ''How'd you...?''

''Never mind that. Tell me about them.''

He narrowed his eyes, and he looked as if he were about to spit at Beau. ''Go to hell.''

Desperation grabbed her stomach as tightly as a clenched belt. Mann wasn't going to tell them anything. He had no reason to care whether or not they stopped whoever it was coming after them. No reason to care whether or not they found their missing daughter.

But Beau wasn't getting out of his chair. He wasn't giving up. He eased back, settling deeper into his seat. His shoulders went slack, and he shed his cop facade. A pensive expression claimed his face and for a long moment he studied Mann. When he spoke, his voice was disarmingly soft. ''My wife's family didn't want her to marry a cop. They didn't think I was good enough for her. Still don't.''

That grabbed Mann's attention, and Deedra felt her own eyes rounding. Her parents had never met Beau. Very likely they never would. And even if they did, whether they approved or disapproved of him would matter little to her or to Beau. But this was just a ploy. A way to make Mann think they had something in common.

''Too bad for you,'' Mann snarled.

Beau wasn't deterred. "I'll bet Merry Sue's folks hated you on sight, too, huh?"

Deedra watched Mann flinch, and then he slumped against the chair back, the mean going out of him. "What'd they know? Bunch a white trash."

"Well, you have to admit you're not exactly the clean-cut all-American boy the average mom and pop dreams their daughter will grow up and marry."

"Hah! Don't go paintin' Merry Sue's kin as no *Brady Bunch*. Pa died afore she were born, and their ma raised the four of 'em on welfare and every other dodge in her bag of tricks."

"So, Merry Sue was the baby of the family." Beau steepled his fingers. His dark eyebrows were low over his green eyes, thoughtful. Insightful. "Then it's likely she was the favorite, wasn't she?"

"You think yer pretty smart, huh?" Mann's watery eyes filled with tears and his voice broke. "Sure she was the favorite. She was pure as rich cream. White-blond hair hangin' down her back. Eyes the blue of an iced-over pond. She wouldn't hurt a critter. Not even a fly. Just shoo it on out of the cabin if it got in."

He put his head in his hands for the beat of two breaths and then lifted tear-filled eyes to Beau. "What'd she ever see in the likes a me?"

Beau winced and swallowed hard. Deedra had a lump in her own throat. She knew Beau's heart went out to the other man for the loss of the woman he'd loved. For the love of the woman he'd lost. She knew he could relate in more ways than Mann would ever learn.

Deedra hugged herself, wishing she could hug Beau instead.

Mann made a face, swiped at his tears, wiped his

nose with his hand, and all the while gazed at Beau with a measuring stare. He tipped his head sideways, then craned his neck. "Yer sorry, ain't you? Not just cause someone's after yer missus, but sorry about Merry Sue and our babe?"

Beau's eyebrows lowered and his expression turned solemn, earnest. No longer cop and killer, now she saw only husband and father talking to husband and father.

"Yes." Beau nodded. "Eternally sorry."

Mann looked as if his throat were thick with emotion. He pressed a fist to his heart. "I like that. Yeah, I do."

Deedra expected he'd laugh that nasty laugh again and tell Beau he hoped he'd choke on the guilt and regret forever. She held her breath as he glanced away, sniffed hard and cleared his throat.

Beau said, "They took my child."

Mann jerked back toward him. His eyes narrowed, and he studied Beau again. "Thought yer little 'un crawled into the woods and—"

"No." Beau interrupted.

Deedra rubbed her fingers gently at her aching temples. She couldn't shake the sense that time was essential. If they couldn't get to these people and soon, they would never find Callie.

"Merry Sue's family took her." Red climbed Beau's neck, and his voice held a dangerous note. "For revenge."

Mann stilled, then shook his head. "An eye for an eye."

Deedra gasped at the reminder of her nightmare. The bull's-eye evolving into mirrored eyes. *An eye for an eye.* Pain throbbed against her skull, matching the ache in her heart.

Mann looked up as if he'd heard her gasp, staring at the mirror as if he could see her. "It ain't right. Snatching a babe from its mama…but it wouldn't be the first time her kin done it."

"What?" Beau lurched out of his chair. "They've done this before?"

"I ain't got proof. But I heared things. Was a rumor goin' 'round Idaho about the time I met Merry Sue."

Beau's brows drew together as though he were dredging an old memory, recalling an old case. "What was your wife's maiden name?"

"Dillard." Mann wiped at his mouth as if he'd just spat something foul. "But that was as changeable as dirty socks. On one day, off the next."

Beau didn't look surprised. "You know any of their aliases?"

He squinted, thinking. "Nash. Bascom. That's the only ones I heared of."

"Where are they?" Beau gave up all pretext of hiding his desperation. "Where do they live?"

"Fer the sake of yer babe, I'd tell ya if'n I knowed." Mann looked as though he meant it. "But they's as hard to pin down as mosquitoes, flittin' in to suck yer blood, then gone before ya can swat 'em. Could be anywheres."

THE DILLARDS might be "anywheres" but as Beau drove Deedra home, getting her promise to rest, he was determined to find them and find out everything he could about them. He tucked Deedra in and kissed her, then stroked near her ear, savoring the silken feel of her short hair and baby-soft skin.

She looked so sad and weary he wanted to climb into the bed with her, hold her and make love to her.

Take all her pain and hurt and heartache into himself. He wanted to bring their little girl home to her and place her in her mother's arms. He leaned down and brushed a kiss to her mouth. "Sleep, my love. I'll be back soon."

"Beau, no." She caught his sleeve. "Not yet. Just hold my hand a moment more, okay?"

"Glad to." He kept his tone and his expression light, striving to hide his distress. He wanted to give her that sense of security she so deserved. "I'm only going to the precinct. To make some calls. See what I can learn about Merry Sue Mann's kin. It's a place to start...."

At long last.

"Then you should go." She stifled a yawn.

"Are you sure?"

"Yes. Go. Find our Callie. You can do it, Beau. I know you can." Her mouth tipped slightly at the corner. The next second her eyelids fluttered shut and her breathing grew easy. There had been a time he would have had to fight for her trust. But she'd given it readily now. The knowledge heartened him. He had to end this nightmare once and for all. He had to find Callie.

He kissed Deedra's forehead. And left.

At the police station, Nora Lee and Heck were at their respective desks, and Nora Lee was on the phone. At this time of day, Luanne had likely gone to her counseling session, which reminded him he would have to deal with Dr. Elle Warren and the missing tapes sometime soon. But he had more pressing concerns right now. First and foremost, protecting Deedra.

He crossed to Heck's desk. "I need you at the ranch to guard Deedra."

"Sure thing, Sheriff." Heck shoved out of the chair.

"I'm on my way." He checked his gun, grabbed his hat and took off, boot heels echoing in his wake.

Nora Lee was still on the phone. Beau checked his own desk for phone messages and then returned to Nora Lee's as he heard her hang up.

He asked, "Was that the lab?"

"No." Nora Lee leaned back in her chair and gazed up at him. "But they did call."

Beau's heart kicked up a beat, and he cautioned himself not to get excited. Or hopeful. It could be bad news. "About Callie's dress?"

She nodded. "I was going to call you, but I wanted to check out something first."

The fact she hadn't called him immediately cooled his jets faster than any talk he'd given himself. The news was not good. "The dress?"

"Oh, sorry. The lab found a speck of blood on the hem. It was *not* Callie's. A DNA match popped up in the data base. A Wanda Dillard. She has a rap sheet that crosses state lines, though she's rarely been convicted."

The Dillards. He supposed he should feel something about having actually gotten confirmation and physical proof. But it put him no closer to finding Callie, and that left him numb. "She's either Merry Sue Mann's mother or a sister."

Nora Lee's ice-blue eyes widened; she blew a low whistle. "I'll be damned. I'd say it's her mother, then. Age fifty. I'm having her mug shot faxed."

"There's a photo of her?" The numbness receded and the first spark of excitement stirred. "How soon will it be here?"

"ASAP. I was hoping to have even more news for you. I just got off with a source I have at the local FBI.

I had him checking to see whether there was a Wanda Dillard listed anywhere in the area. He found an address, but said it came up bogus.''

"Figures." He propped himself on her desk, arms stiff and palms flat. "Think your source would also check out Wanda Nash and Wanda Bascom?"

"Aliases?"

"Yeah."

"I'll call him."

The outer door banged open, and Luanne stormed in, cursing under her breath. "Talk about unprofessional. She really takes the cake."

"Dr. Warren?" Nora said in a disinterested tone, swinging toward the phone as if anxious not to get into this conversation.

"Who else?" Luanne's glasses were steamed, her brown curls wild. "You know, if I don't show up for an appointment, my insurance won't pay her but *she charges me.* And I work hard for my money. But when she doesn't show up, what am I supposed to do? Send her a bill?"

Beau felt as if someone held an icicle against his spine.

"Dr. Warren didn't show up for your appointment?"

"No. And she didn't call and reschedule, either. In fact, her office is locked and dark, all the blinds drawn."

Nora Lee stopped with the receiver halfway to her ear. "That doesn't sound like Dr. Warren. You can usually set your watch by her schedule."

Beau agreed. She was obsessive to a fault. His gut pinched, and he tried telling himself it had nothing to do with Deedra's stolen tapes. But he feared it did. "Make your call, Nora Lee. I'll check on the doctor."

He hurried to his office, looked up the doctor's home and office numbers. He tried her home first. No answer. The machine wasn't turned on. Odd. He dialed her office number. After five rings he reached her voice mail. The outgoing message said she'd closed for the day, but would be in by nine in the morning. It was yesterday's tape.

He cursed. His mind conjured nasty scenarios and he prayed he was jumping to conclusions. That she'd had a family emergency or something equally unexpected that hadn't left her time to notify anyone. But she wasn't the type to leave her patients hanging. He ran stiffly on his sore leg into the booking area. "Nora Lee, come with me. Luanne, stay here and catch the phones."

Nora Lee waited until they were in the cruiser. "What's happening? Where are we going?"

"To Dr. Warren's office. I have a nasty feeling in my gut, and I hope to hell I'm wrong." He explained about the doctor's call, about the missing tapes, about the doctor deciding she didn't want him nosing into her files. That *she* would handle it. "I shouldn't have listened to her. Should have insisted, but with all that's been going on with Deedra and Callie and..."

"Don't beat yourself up, Sheriff. Not much you could do if she wouldn't cooperate."

He knew that. But maybe if he'd followed through... The thought scattered as he skidded to a stop in front of the doctor's office. Closed blinds covered the windows. Even in the waiting area, and Dr. Warren never closed those. The pinching in his gut sharpened.

He climbed the porch, Nora Lee right beside him. She took a position on one side of the door, he on the other. He tried the knob. "Locked," he said, and added a cautioning, "Stand back."

He lifted his good leg and rammed his boot heel into the door below the knob. Once. Twice. Wood cracked. He kicked harder. The bolt gave in a wrenching clank and the door bounced inward. The waiting room was as dark as the secrets of Dr. Warren's patients.

Beau drew his weapon from its holster, flicked off the safety and saw Nora Lee had done the same. "Ready?"

She nodded. He entered first. Nora Lee followed. He found a switch. Darkness fled in a glare of bright overhead light. He blinked against the sudden change of focus. Nora Lee checked behind the door, while he moved into the waiting area, gun barrel pointed at the ceiling. His eyes took in every inch of the room. He called, "Dr. Warren, are you here?"

The waiting area held a love seat and two chairs, chosen, he suspected for their uncluttered lines and nonthreatening hues. Plants stood sentinel near the two front windows. Unlike a medical doctor who booked quick appointment after quick appointment, Dr. Warren saw one patient every hour. The visits lasted fifty minutes, assuring no runover of folk to fill her waiting room.

"Dr. Warren?"

Flies circled in the still air. On cat feet, Beau crept toward the end of the room, noting no one had dusted the glass-top tables or straightened magazines or wiped away fingerprint smudges. He doubted the latents left behind would do more than identify the last patients she'd seen yesterday. He called again, "Dr. Warren?"

As he neared the end of the room, he caught it...a familiar sickly sweet stench that made his stomach churn. The smell of death. His heart wrenched. He stopped Nora Lee in her tracks. "You check out her office, I'll do this room."

Nora Lee did as directed. "The door's locked."

"Then leave it be…for now. And call the M.E."

Surprise filled her voice, "The medical examin— You mean, she's dead?"

"Someone sure as hell is." He tried the door. Unlocked. The stench was intense and he hesitated, knowing what awaited him. Dreading it.

He braced himself and shoved the door inward. The buzz of flies was thick here, colliding with a rhythmic static that echoed through the darkness. He groped for the wall switch. Light stroked over the exercise stand, the minifridge, the half-full bottle of water on its top, and the fly-littered body on the floor. The odor slammed into his nostrils and he reeled back, his gaze glued on Dr. Elle Warren.

It was the first time he'd ever seen her long sandy hair mussed, he realized. It had come free of its band and spilled over the hefty base of the bench's metal framework, half hiding the doctor's face. There was no mistaking the identity of the rusty fluid pooled beneath her head. Dried blood.

Damn it. Damned woman. Why hadn't she let him help?

A Walkman was hooked on the waistband of her workout shorts, and the headset rested near her knee. Static radio music blared from each earphone.

"M.E.'s on his way." Nora Lee came up behind him, her hand on her nose, her eyes wide with horror. "Oh, God."

"Yeah," Beau agreed. He expected she might be sick, but though her eyes remained wide and her skin had paled, she didn't run out. She hadn't gotten ill at Nell Carter's either, reacting less like a rookie and more like an old hand at homicide, and he wondered where and when she'd faced her first dead body.

"Was it an accident?"

"Maybe. Maybe not. Just in case, don't come in. And don't touch anything."

"Of course not."

"Use your cell phone and get the crime lab over here, too."

As she made the call, he scanned the room again. The nasty buzz of the flies mixed with the static beat from the earphones scraped against his nerves. He forced his concentration to the doctor. One hand was outstretched, her index finger covered in blood. He studied the floor near it. Had she been trying to print something…in her own blood?

Stepping with care, he inched closer. It looked like a letter, but he couldn't be sure. He crouched down for a better slant and flies came to investigate the newcomer. He batted them from his eyes. Cursing. Here the static music was louder, too, more irritating.

He reached to shut off the Walkman and froze. The edge of an envelope poked out from under the headset. His pulse lurched to the rhythm issuing from the small radio. He shouldn't touch the envelope. But he knew he had to. Knew it was for him.

Pinching the edge, he tugged it from beneath her. His mouth dried. His name was on it, written with the familiar hated curlicued E. He didn't even try to be careful. Just tore open the flap.

"Sheriff?"

Beau jerked and glanced over his shoulder.

Nora Lee's face registered shock, as though she couldn't believe he was contaminating a crime scene.

"It's from the sniper," he said. "Wanda Dillard. Another note. Left for me. Probably about Callie."

The shock dissolved into a look of understanding. "What does it say?"

He withdrew the single sheet of paper, and read:

"Oh where, oh where can your Callie be?
You can't find her and you can't find me.
But this game's no fun, if you don't play.
So I left you a clue in Mann's cabin today."

"Wow." Nora Lee exclaimed. "What a heartless bitch."

Beau reared up from his haunches. His heart seemed ready to explode. He had to calm down. Had to think.

"You aren't going there alone," Nora Lee said. "You know it's probably a trap."

"Probably." He gestured toward the dead psychologist. "But this can't wait and someone has to stay here and handle the lab and the M.E. I'm counting on you to do that."

"Then take Heck."

"No. I don't want Deedra left without a guard."

"Then be careful."

"Don't worry. That I will be." He went outside to the car, sucking in the fresh air, hot and cleansing. The M.E.'s wagon pulled up beside his car as he sank onto the seat and phoned the ranch. Pilar answered and he asked for his deputy. When Heck came on the line he assured Beau that Deedra was still asleep.

Beau said, "I've received another note from the sniper. She's supposedly left me a clue to Callie's whereabouts at Floyd Mann's cabin. I'm going up there and get it.''

"Nora Lee's going with you, ain't she?''

"No.''

"Then I'll be right there. Wait for me.''

"No. Stay where you are. I don't want Deedra left alone and vulnerable.''

"Then take Nora Lee. She's good with a gun and sharp-witted to boot. Couldn't ask for better backup.''

"I can't. She has to stay here and handle the details of Dr. Warren's…death.''

"The doc's dead? But she was healthy as a horse.'' Heck hesitated, belatedly realizing that if the doctor had died of natural causes, there would be no reason for Nora Lee to see to the details. "You sayin' she was murdered?''

Beau explained. He and Heck rang off, hanging up in sync.

In the upstairs bedroom, Deedra replaced the receiver in its cradle. Her heart skipped along at an alarming rate. She flew off the bed and tossed on clothes. Beau was *not* going to Mann's cabin alone.

Chapter Nineteen

"Shanahan's not here yet."

"Good. But he will be soon. And I imagine the first thing he'll do is secure the perimeter. Make sure no one's waitin' in ambush."

"Agreed. We can't take up position anywhere around the cabin until he's inside."

"Let's beat it back to the car. Won't do to get caught standin' here jawin' when he drives in."

"Right. We can see the lane from where we parked, and he won't see us."

Once they were inside the car the discussion began again. "There he goes. We'll give him a good five minutes, let him get inside."

Anticipation crammed the interior of the concealed car. The people crouched inside felt the culmination of all their lying schemes and risky deeds coming to a head. But they knew not to get too cocky.

Nothing ever went exactly as planned.

BEAU PLANNED TO SURVIVE. To get the clue to Callie's whereabouts and come away from here intact. He backed his car into a pull-off, going in deeply enough to conceal the cruiser but leaving himself ease for a fast getaway.

As he raced up the lane, he felt keyed up. He fought the urge to rush inside the cabin. He palmed his gun and studied the ramshackle structure from a secure spot in the underbrush.

It looked deserted. But no one knew better than Beau how deceiving looks could be. Hate spread over his heart like a dark shadow. "Are you in there?" he whispered. "Just waiting for me?"

He crept through the underbrush as quietly as the wind, every step on the rocky ground no noisier than a rattler slithering through a dry river bed. If she *was* in there, he wanted her. Wanted her alive more than he would have ever thought possible.

He'd kicked the door in last time he was here. It still hung off its hinges. He watched for several heart-trembling minutes. Nothing moved behind the splintered wood. It made him feel no better. She might be in the other room. Might be as patient and as cautious as he.

He circled the cabin. Once. Twice. Startled birds took flight. Squirrels skittered. Bees buzzed in wildflowers. But he saw no movement from behind the windows.

Maybe she was outside. Watching him.

A shiver scurried across his flesh. He stepped with the caution of a lamb being stalked by a cougar. He sensed the predator but he couldn't see her. One misstep and it could all go wrong. So wrong…

He couldn't crouch here waiting for something to happen. He had to see what she'd left him in that cabin. The clue that would lead him to Callie. He rose up off his haunches and tightened his grip on his gun. Sweat slid beneath his Kevlar vest to settle in the small of his back. "It's now or never, Shanahan."

He ran in a zigzag pattern to the porch. No one fired at him. He flattened himself against the building. His chest rose and fell in fast bumps. He waited two minutes. He shoved through the broken door. Without stopping to do more than peruse the main room, he rushed to the bedroom.

Through the murky light he saw that the closet door stood open, as did the hatch cover to the hidey-hole. A dark stain smeared the wooden slats where he'd fallen after being shot by Mann. His blood. A pang of pain stabbed his knee as if in remembrance. He drew a shuddery breath, pulling in the stink of cold wood fires and bacon fat.

He was alone. But for how long? He needed to find what she'd left and get the hell out of here. His gaze landed on the cradle. Something poked from beneath the baby blanket and he recoiled as he remembered the awful encounter with the rubber doll. He shook himself and strode back to the main room.

His eyes had begun to adjust to the shadowy light. He held his back against the doorjamb. It gave him the advantage of seeing both rooms at once. And it gave him the upper hand should he need to get out fast.

Rat droppings and critter paw prints disturbed the dust coating the pinochle-size table, its two straight-back chairs, the rockers and the sideboard. But there was nothing left by any human vermin. He shifted his gaze across the stove and the shelves above. Nothing.

The rumble of a motor outside galvanized him. His heart boomed. Who was it? Her? He raced to the window. As he realized whose car it was and who was inside it, he swore. His fear jumping notches higher than before.

He ran to the porch, confronting Deedra and Heck as they hurried toward him. "Get down." He swore. "Keep down."

He caught her hand and pulled her into the cabin. "Damn it, Dee, you shouldn't be here. It's too dangerous."

She snapped back. "It's too dangerous for you to be here alone."

He shook his head. Knowing it was a waste of time arguing with his stubborn, beautiful wife, he turned and glared at his deputy. "What the hell were you thinking bringing her here? I told you to stay with her at the ranch. Can't you follow a simple order?"

Cowed, Heck glanced at Deedra. "I told you he'd skin me alive for bringin' you to this place."

"Don't be upset with Heck, Beau. The phone woke me, and I listened in on your conversation. I heard about Dr. Warren, and I wasn't about to let you walk into a trap. Most certainly not alone. Your deputy came along to protect me and help you, if need be."

Scowling, he stepped back to the door and again scanned the perimeter. He didn't see anyone, but the hair on his nape prickled. The sensation of someone watching.

"I don't like this, Dee. I wish you hadn't come." His gaze pinned Heck. "And you and I will discuss it later."

"Have you found it yet?" Deedra gazed around the room, hugging herself. Purple underscored her eyes, and the lines around her mouth were drawn taut. "The clue about Callie?"

"No. But I just started looking. I don't think it's in this room."

"The other room?" Deedra glanced at the open jamb and started for it. Beau followed, feeling the inexplicable sense that he should stay as close to Deedra as he could. He watched her take in the room, the hidey-hole, the dark stain. Saw her put it together. Realize it was his blood on that spot. She trembled but gazed at the trap door. "What's down there?"

"A cellar of sorts. Dug from the soil."

She nodded and stepped to the closet, looked inside. "How about up there?"

"Bat guano."

Deedra stepped back and spun toward him but stayed at the closet. She studied the bedroom, and Beau again felt the creeping sense that he shouldn't allow any distance between them. Even a short one. He moved to her side.

Heck hung in the doorway, as Beau had done earlier, keeping watch in both directions, his gun drawn, the barrel pointed at the floor. But Beau recognized the tense set of his shoulders. He was as alert as a bloodhound.

"Beau," Deedra called. "What's that?"

She was pointing to the baby cradle. An errant ray of sun bore through the dusty window like a spotlight, highlighting something poking out from under the blanket. He'd assumed earlier that it was the rubber doll. But he saw now it was fuzzy and pink with white grosgrain. It looked like...

"Callie's bunny!" Deedra sobbed and hurried to it. She dropped to her knees, scooped the toy from beneath the blankets and hugged it to her.

Beau squatted beside her and pulled her into his

arms. She trembled in his embrace, and the sense of danger increased, wrapping him as tightly as he enfolded her. They couldn't stay here. "Dee, is there a note pinned to the bunny?"

She pulled back and lowered the toy away from her chest. There was nothing there. Something niggled in the back of Beau's mind. Last time he'd seen this stuffed toy was with the other things from the accident scene stored in the evidence room. "Was this bunny in your case file box the day you were looking at the crime-scene photos?"

"No."

"How'd it get here?"

"I put it there," a voice behind them said.

They lurched around toward the doorway. Heck held his gun trained on Deedra. "Drop your gun, Beau, or she's dead."

He had Deedra directly in his sights. Beau could get off a shot, but so could Heck. He couldn't risk it. He laid his gun by his foot, slowly rose and put Deedra behind him, shielding her. "Why would you—"

"Merry Sue was my sister, and her baby was to be my niece."

Beau felt as if he'd been shot in the gut. He'd trusted this man. Trusted him with his life. With Deedra's life. And all the while the bastard... Beau's hands curled into fists. "You son of a bit—"

"Uh, uh, uh." Heck waved his gun. "The second I shoot you, I'll go after yer missus. That whatcha want?"

"You like shooting women, don't you?" Deedra spat.

"Always a crack shot. Ma taught me. And when

some woman needs shuttin' up, like Freddie Carter's old lady and that mouthy shrink, I'm willin' to step up.''

''We thought a woman was doing this.'' Confusion rang in Deedra's voice. ''Were you the one sending notes to Beau?''

''Ma did that. She hates Beau real bad.''

''Where's my daughter, you bastard?'' Beau felt his blood pressure spiking.

''Where you'll never find her.''

Beau charged him. Heck fired the gun, missing him by inches. But as Beau ducked, Heck slammed the butt of the gun against his temple. Pain radiated from the contact point. Stars danced before his eyes. He felt himself toppling toward the cellar. He reached out to stop himself, but his hands met empty air. And as he dropped into the pit, blackness engulfing him, he heard Deedra scream his name.

Then nothing.

''BEAU!'' DEEDRA RACED to the pit. ''Beau! Answer me!''

''There's a ladder,'' Heck said. ''Find it and join your husband.''

Deedra felt the barrel of the gun press against her temple. She gazed up into his cold eyes and knew he had no compassion. He would kill both her and Beau if she joined her husband in the cellar. She also knew that he would drop her where she knelt and kick her into the hole on top of Beau if she disobeyed. Hoping to buy some time and needing to help Beau, she groped for the ladder and hurried down, never taking her eyes from the man with the gun. Fear galloped in her chest. Dampness surrounded her like a shroud. She felt the ground for Beau.

"Ain't that sweet? Instead of running away, you're finally running to yer hubby." He kicked Callie's bunny into the hole. "Now that it's too late."

He began lowering the hatch cover. Deedra pleaded, "Please, don't do this."

"Save your breath. It's all but done."

"Just tell me, is Callie alive?" Deedra begged, "Please, I need to know."

Heck squatted down and peered at her, grinning viciously. "She's alive, but she'll never know she's a Shanahan. An eye for an eye. A daughter for a daughter. A baby for a baby."

He slammed the hatch, casting her in utter darkness. She heard something scrape across the floor and figured it was the bed. She felt for and found Beau, and then she sat and gathered his head into her lap. "Beau?"

He was breathing, but she couldn't see him or tell how badly he was hurt.

Her lower back began to ache. Then a sudden cramp slashed her belly. *Oh, God, no. Not now. Not here.* She needed to help Beau. Needed to· get them out of this trap. Overhead, Heck's footsteps retreated, then returned. Seconds later she made out the sound of something sloshing against the floor. The biting stench flared into her nose. Gasoline.

"Beau! Beau!" She shook him, terror hot in her veins. "Oh, God, please, Beau, wake up!"

A loud whoosh. A startling roar. Then the crackle of burning wood.

Deedra couldn't move. Couldn't breathe. Her limbs had gone limp with terror. Her lower body cramped, bending her double with the vicious pain. The first whiff of smoke seared through her, wiping out all else but the instinct to survive. She lowered Beau's head to the packed dirt floor and laid Callie's bunny on his chest.

He gave a soft moan as she scrambled up the ladder. She found the bottom of the trap door. It felt warm. She levered her shoulder against it and shoved upward with all her might.

It didn't move. She pushed again. And again. Sucking in air. Smoke. She began to feel light-headed. Somewhere beyond the pain and dizziness, she caught the sound of gunfire. Help was coming.

But she knew it would be too late.

Chapter Twenty

Beau screwed his eyes open. A band of light was bearing down on him from what looked like a tunnel. Was he dead, heading into that bright neon of eternity? The beam came closer and began to sting his eyes. He blinked and looked away. The air tasted thick. Smoky. Maybe he wasn't headed for Heaven, but for hell.

He coughed hard. Pain zinged across his skull and ricocheted around his head like a wizard's pinball. God, what was wrong with him? Where was he? He thought he heard voices behind the light, but a horrible roaring from overhead drowned out the actual words. His eyes watered, blurring his vision. Now there were several lights. Bobbing toward him. He groaned and tried to sit up, but something had him pinned. A dead weight on his chest.

"They're here!"

The shout startled him. The next second, the weight lifted off his chest and he saw it was Deedra. Hanging limp in the arms of a stranger. His heart chilled. "No! Dee!"

The words choked out of his raspy throat and dissolved in a fit of coughs.

"It's okay," said one the voices near his ear. Hands

grasped under his armpits. "We're FBI, Sheriff. You and your wife are lucky we found the back way into this cellar. It hasn't been used in so long, we had a hell of a time getting it open."

Not Heaven. Not hell. The cellar in Mann's cabin. Not dead. Just feeling like it.

"We have to go *now*, Sheriff!" They hauled him to his feet. "Can you walk?"

"I—" He retched on his shoes.

The agents swore but pulled him ahead. Beau staggered along, feeling woozy—as drunk as a rodeo clown. Pain resonated in every molecule of his being, and fear for Deedra had a half nelson on his heart.

The two agents, whose faces he couldn't see, grunted under his weight. But they kept him moving. Behind him, a crackling whoosh sounded.

"Hurry!" one of the agents hollered. "That floor's about to collapse…and send the fire roaring through the tunnel after us!"

Coughing and limping, his bad leg feeling shattered, Beau emerged into the night with the help of his saviors. "Dee—" he croaked. "Where—"

"The lady's on her way to the hospital!" one of the agents shouted above the roar to his back.

Beau turned toward the unnatural light rebounding off the forest walls and his heart seized. The spot where Mann's cabin had stood was now a bonfire gone bad. Kindling-dry wood crackled and snapped and collapsed in on itself, shooting sparks and tongues of fire lancing toward treetops. They were lucky to have gotten out alive. But until he knew Dee was safe…

The FBI agents handed Beau over to a strapping EMT, a man surprisingly bigger than Beau.

"Wife—" he asked the medical man, but the one

word was all he got out as an oxygen mask snapped over his mouth and nose.

"Breathe," the EMT directed. He helped Beau into the ambulance, but as he tried strapping him onto a cot both of them noticed the blood on his jeans and shirt. "Oh, God, you're bleeding!"

"I am?" Beau hurt so much all over he couldn't distinguish any one area of pain from another.

The EMT cut off Beau's clothes, but there were no open gashes or wounds. He handed him a blanket. "You've got a few contusions, but nothing to explain the blood."

Dee's blood? Had Heck shot her? Oh, God, no! "My wife…is it her blood?" He wrapped the blanket around his waist.

"Sir, please, breathe." The EMT put the mask on Beau again.

Beau wrenched it off. "Damn it! Find out!"

"Your wife was conscious when she left, but that's all I know. You'll be at the hospital soon, and we'll be able to check on her condition then. Okay?"

"No. Call now."

"I'll call as soon as you let me check your vitals." The ambulance doors banged shut and the vehicle began moving. The EMT pressed him to sit.

Beau glared at the man for a full five seconds, but in the end knew he was just wasting time. He lay down, accepted the mask and drew a deep breath of the rich oxygen, silently willing the man to hurry with his examination. He prayed for Dee, prayed she hadn't been shot. But he kept seeing her limp body being carried out of the cellar, and his fear reached higher than the sparks in the night sky, pushing terror through him with the force of a backlash.

"That's a nasty bruise on your temple," the EMT commented. "Are you seeing double?"

Was he? His eyes stung and watered. A racking cough climbed his throat and exploded against the oxygen mask, pulsing pain through his head until he thought his skull would crack open. *Oh, damn it. He was going to be sick again.* He cursed, and his world went black.

THE MOMENT BEAU OPENED his eyes, he threw up again. But he had arrived at the hospital. He refused treatment until he knew Deedra's condition. Dr. Haynes informed him that Deedra appeared to have ingested an insubstantial amount of smoke. They were running a blood-gas test. She hadn't been shot. The bleeding was a side effect of her pending condition. Once they knew whether or not her oxygen levels were normal, and as soon as her surgeon arrived, she would have that long-put-off hysterectomy.

The news was better than he'd hoped and worse in some ways. He didn't care that Dee could not bear him another child. He wanted her alive and well and beyond the pain she'd been putting up with for far too long. He just wanted her any way he could have her. But he recalled her distress over Sean's statement that he should have "big scrappin' sons" to carry on the Shanahan heritage. Deedra had let that bruise her soul.

Once the surgeon had cut out that part of her that a lot of women considered to be what made them women, she might be devastated. If she was convinced he no longer wanted her for herself alone, she would reject him before he could reject her. For he knew she'd always held back a part of her heart. And he knew if she continued to do that, then they might have no future. Somehow he had to make her see that she was his other half, that without her he might as well be dead.

With that unhappy thought, he drifted off.

HE AWOKE AGAIN to find himself in a bed that felt too narrow and too short for his bulk and frame. He no longer wore the oxygen mask, and he could smell antiseptic without the lingering stench of smoke. His leg was wrapped tight and his head hurt like hell. Various other aches and pains remained unidentified.

A nurse was fiddling with an IV. He recognized the thick golden braid against her back. "Cassidy, is that you?"

"Ah, you're awake. How's your head feel?"

"Like it was trampled by a wild bronc. How's Dee?"

"In surgery, but she should be out soon. As much as I could find out, it was textbook. So she should be fine, Beau."

"Thank you." He eased back, his head pounding. But would *they* be fine?

"You, on the other hand," Cassidy said cheerily. "Have a really ugly bruise at your temple, one whale of a concussion, and a wrenched knee in the leg that was healing."

"At least I know why I feel this bad."

"The good news is, your blood gasses are normal now."

"You feeling up to company?" A woman's voice brought his gaze to the door. He had to look twice before he realized it was the adoption attorney, the last person he would expect to show up in his hospital room. Though she appeared as unlike the person he'd met in her office as she could get.

"I'll go check on Deedra for you," Cassidy said and left.

"Thanks," Beau called after her.

As T.R. came toward him, Beau assessed her appearance. Instead of her usual designer suit, the beautiful brunette looked like what she'd claimed to be: a born-and-bred Montana girl. She wore cowboy boots beneath tight jeans, her hair in a ponytail. But it was the surprising blue windbreaker that had him rubbing at his eyes.

She laughed. "You're not seeing things, Sheriff Shanahan."

"*You're* FBI?" His voice rasped.

"Special Agent T. R. Rudway." Soot and dirt smudged her cheeks and chin. "Sorry about the deception, but it was necessary. The bogus office was decorated upscale so it would be sure to discourage the locals from seeking my services."

"What about the pregnant teen and the Southern couple Deedra encountered who were adopting her baby?"

"All three are agents working undercover with me."

"I thought your 'history' was too slick." Beau frowned, then winced at the pain that small gesture brought banging through his skull. "In fact, I told Dee that. After calling the list of names you'd given me, I sensed something was wrong. That it was just too pat. But I never suspected this. Your act *was* convincing."

"The fear was easy. I figured you'd sniff me out in seconds if you got too close and I just used that fear to my best advantage. I couldn't have you blowing my cover. I've been after Wanda Dillard for over a year now. The rumors of her snatching children and crossing state lines with them isn't just rumor.''

Hope spread through him, but he feared that hope. It might destroy him. ''Did you get her?''

Did you find Callie?

''When Special Agent Anderson—I believe you know her as Nora Lee—informed me that you were headed to Mann's cabin alone, *you* became a priority.''

''Wait a minute. Nora Lee is FBI, too?'' He supposed *that* made a certain sense, given her connection with the local FBI and her poise at murder scenes.

''Sure is. She and I figured you were heading into a trap. We were at Mann's cabin before you. You see, some time ago, we discovered Heck Long was actually Hank Dillard. We've been keeping tabs on him ever since.''

''But Nora Lee suggested I bring him along as backup.''

''We thought Wanda might be the one waiting to spring her trap on you and had hoped to catch her and Heck in one fell swoop.''

But Wanda hadn't been there. He lay back on his pillow and closed his eyes against the pain rolling behind his eyeballs, taking in all the new information.

T.R. kept talking, filling the tense gaps in conversation. ''Wanda's cagey. Last time we had a lead on her, she disappeared. When she resurfaced, she'd disposed of the child.''

''Dis—'' Beau's heart lurched, and his face drained of heat. ''Dead?''

''No, no.'' She held up her hands, trying to take the edge off his fear. ''Put up for adoption. Illegal, of course. All the papers forged. Unfortunately, the adoptive parents didn't know until they'd fallen in love with the child. Fortunately, the real parents have their little boy back now.''

Beau's chest loosened a bit, and he reached for that hope again. Hope that Callie could be, would be found. But he couldn't bear to put that hope into words and have it dashed.

''You should know that we were also keeping an eye on Luanne Pine.'' She rubbed at her cheek, hitting a spot of soot and smearing it. ''Her mother, Ivy, is Wanda Dillard's sister.''

The news dropped Beau's jaw. He felt like an idiot. No one in his office was who or what they appeared. ''Luanne was involved in Callie's—''

''That's the interesting part. Ivy and Luanne are innocent dupes. Merry Sue was Luanne's cousin and best friend. She's taken Merry Sue's death hard enough to need counseling to work through it. But she has never sought vengeance. Never blamed you. Had no idea what her aunt Wanda and cousin Heck were really up to. But she didn't inform you they were related because Heck warned her not to. He told her you hated nepotism and you'd fire one of them if you knew they were cousins. And it wouldn't be him. She needed the job so she kept his secret.''

''What about her mother?''

''Ivy runs a day care, but Wanda told Luanne and Ivy that she was taking in foster kids from time to time. They believed her.''

His hope leaped with new legs. ''You think one of those so-called foster kids may be Callie?''

''We did.''

Did. The word spread ice across his lungs, froze his hope and shattered it like ice crystals against stone. He couldn't drag in a breath. "Then you've located Wanda Dillard?"

"In custody." Her face held no sunshine, just a weary darkness. He wanted to step back from the pain that was coming, knowing it would be worse than anything he'd already suffered. "Agents were going in at about the same time we were rescuing you and Mrs. Shanahan from that cellar. They found two children living in her home. Both boys. Not Callie."

She said the last with compassion, but no matter how soft her words, they chiseled through his heart. He couldn't hold in a sob.

"We're not giving up, Beau. We'll keep looking for your daughter no matter how long it takes."

He nodded and she knew he needed to be alone. The door closed and the silence wrapped around him. Hurt settled in his chest, a hard, hot ball of wounded despair. How could he tell Dee?

DEEDRA'S MOUTH FELT COTTONY, her shoulder tender and sore. She moved and winced, identifying a different area of distress. Her lower body. But this ache was an ache dulled by pain killer. Why had no one ever invented painkiller for heartache? For loss? A pill or serum that would deaden emotional agony? For no matter how hard she'd tried not to, she kept hearing Heck telling her they'd never see Callie again.

She drew a wobbly breath and caught a scent she recognized beneath the antiseptic ruling the air near her nose. Not cologne. Not man-made. But of the man. A scent unique to him.

Beau.

His handsome face, battered and bruised, hovered inches from her own. Her pulse hummed at the sight of him, and a smile sprang to her lips. He sucked in a breath as if every part of him were in pain. She wanted to fold him to her, but she was strapped down with IV tubes, and he balanced on crutches. She settled for caressing his cheek below the purplish discoloration. "Does it hurt much?"

His mouth softened. "I was going to ask you that."

"Oh. Well…I have great drugs. But with a concussion you're probably not on anything yet."

"You're right."

"Did they catch Heck?"

"No one told you?"

She shook her head. "You tell me."

She patted the bed, inching over slightly so that he could sit beside her. She wanted him near. No more distance between them. Not right now. Beau settled with care, putting the crutches to rest against a visitor's chair and taking her hand in his. He filled her in on all that T. R. Rudway had told him about herself, Nora Lee and the Dillard family.

"Callie?"

He glanced away from her, blowing a breath through his nostrils, and when his gaze locked with hers a second later, a sheen slicked his eyes. His grip tightened on her hand and his voice cracked as he said, "I'm sorry, Dee. She wasn't one of the children at Wanda Dillard's house."

Deedra had braced for this eventuality, but still tears stung her eyes and threatened to spill hot and scalding down her cheeks. She blinked hard. She would *not* cry. She would not fall apart and deepen Beau's pain. *But, oh God, Callie.* She swallowed with difficulty, and counted herself lucky to have Beau. She hadn't felt his support when Callie had disappeared, but she had it now. She knew now that he felt the same exact loss and ache she did, and somehow that eased her suffering. They could get through this together. If he was willing.

"T.R. thinks she may have already been adopted by someone," he said, sounding as if he'd abandoned all but the smallest of hope. "If that's so, she says there will be a paper trail and our chances of finding Callie will increase."

Deedra inhaled once. Twice. She needed courage to broach her next question. Courage to face his answer if it was not what she hoped. She'd planned to leave once she'd had her surgery, but in the cellar she'd realized she would rather die with Beau than live without him.

He was her other half. Callie had come into their lives as a gift, an extension of their love, but she wasn't the main element of it. That precious commodity belonged to Beau and her alone.

She finger-combed her hair, thinking suddenly that she likely looked a fright. "What if you *knew* we would never find Callie, Beau? I mean, what Sean said about you having 'scrappin' Shanahan sons'...well, you're a great daddy and you should have kids. Lots of kids."

Beau touched her face as if she were the most delicate lace, the most treasured jewel. "I don't need children to fulfill me, Dee. I need you. Only you. As long as I have your heart, I'll be one happy cowboy."

"You have my heart, Beau. All of it."

"Welcome home, Dee." He grinned and leaned to kiss her, his mouth sealing their deal better than any handshake or contract.

"I hate to interrupt this tender moment..." Cassidy

barged into the room. "But I'm glad to find you both together. Sean is coming. We have a surprise for you."

Surprise? What Deedra would rather have is a few moments alone with her husband. She struggled to keep her face from showing her annoyance at the ill-timed intrusion.

Beau gathered his composure with difficulty and Deedra did the same. He held tight to her hand and grinned at Cassidy. "What's this? You finally get him to pop the question?"

"Not yet, but I'm working on it." Cassidy gave a flip of her braid. She looked shaken to her toes but excited. "This is even bigger than that."

Deedra frowned, her curiosity raging. "How so?"

"I'll let Sean tell you." The door opened and Sean's silver crewcut poked through. Cassidy turned back toward Deedra and Beau, grinning sloppily. "Or should I say, I'll let him show you?"

A little boy with dirty-blond hair cut close to his head, clung to Sean's neck. The child looked about two years old, dressed for play in a colorful T-shirt, faded jeans and scuffed tennis shoes.

Beau shifted on the bed, and Deedra winced at the sharp zing of pain his movement caused across her belly, but she couldn't take her gaze off Sean. If she didn't know better she'd think his eyelashes were damp. His cheeks, too. Inexplicably her heart began to beat a tattoo and her mouth went drier than desert air.

"What is this, Sean?" Beau demanded. "If you've come up with some scheme or other about Deedra and me adopting a child—"

"Why don't you shut up?" Sean barked. "And open your eyes, son?"

The little boy lifted his head, and Beau stopped

speaking as he saw the child's face. Deedra and he said it at the same time, "Callie!"

Her long raven hair had been cropped and bleached, but there was no mistaking those raven-lashed, green eyes. Beau's eyes. Beau shook as he reached for his daughter. Sean grasped his arm, and tears filled the older Shanahan's eyes. "We got our little girl back, Beau. We got her back."

Callie came reluctantly into her daddy's arms, and her daddy closed his eyes as though he couldn't bear the joy.

Seconds ago Deedra had accepted that they might never see their child again. And now, in the blink of God's eye, here she was. She reached a trembling hand to touch her baby, and tears burned through her eyes. Blurred her vision. For the first time in longer than she could recall, she let go and wept, rejoicing in this miracle. Tears streamed hot against her cheeks, tasting salty in her mouth.

But Callie couldn't know she cried for happiness. The tears might be scaring her. Deedra swiped at them and smiled at the little girl whose face had haunted her dreams. Callie's eyes were wide, her raven lashes blinking quickly. Her eyebrows had been left their natural black, and the roots of her hair were still ebony. A sprinkling of freckles had started popping up on her button nose. There was a tiny white scar on the underside of her chin. It hadn't been there before….

Deedra touched it with her finger, and Callie shied away. Pulled back. Deedra hesitated, then caressed her daughter's tiny, perfect fingers, and this time Callie grabbed on to her hand. Fascinated by her wedding ring.

Cassidy and Sean had slipped out of the room, leaving the small family to reunite. Beau and she couldn't get enough of touching Callie, talking to her. After a while a look came into Callie's eyes, a recognition of Deedra and Beau that was primal but indecipherable by a toddler's mind.

Deedra kept her touches light, her voice lighter. It would take time to make their daughter feel secure again. Before she would really "know" her mommy and daddy.

"Her hair's as short as yours," Beau laughed.

"It'll grow." Deedra laughed, reaching for her own hair. "Six months from now we'll both have long hair again."

"I hate to intrude on this happy reunion," Deedra's surgeon said as he did just that. "Are you two ready for more good news?"

Beau stroked his daughter's hair. "Doctor, there couldn't be news better than this."

Epilogue

Six Months Later

The barn of the S bar S pulsed with voices and music and celebration the likes of which Buffalo Falls hadn't enjoyed in years. Cassidy Brewer had finally hooked and landed Sean Shanahan and thrown a wedding and reception with guests including everyone in town.

Pilar had catered the shindig and outdone herself. Beau stood beside his uncle, watching Cassidy, a vision in off-white, her golden hair loose and swinging as she danced with her brother. Beau would swear his uncle hadn't stopped grinning since he'd said, "I do."

He clasped Sean's shoulder, nodding his head toward Cassidy. "Now *that* is a Shanahan woman if ever I saw one."

"You would be the expert in that area." Sean said it as a compliment. He'd finally welcomed Deedra into the family with open arms, but she'd also, finally, included herself in the family.

Beau teased. "Took you long enough to come to your senses."

"Took Cassidy tossin' out her birth control," he whispered. "Hell, I couldn't let my own child be born out of wedlock. Now I'm worried the whole town's gonna know it when the baby comes early.''

Beau laughed. ''It's your own damned fault. If you'd admitted to yourself *and her* sooner that you're head-over-heels and always have been, you'd have saved yourself that indignity. But you always were as stubborn as six mules.''

Sean let off a braying laugh, sounding like the very animals in question. ''Yeah, I guess I'll just have to settle for a lifetime of pure old happiness.''

''I guess you will.''

Cassidy came to retrieve her groom. ''I need to sit down and have some punch.'' She fanned herself. ''For a January night, it's hotter than Hades in here.''

Sean was as delicate with her as he could be tough with a wild bronco. He led his bride to a table, kissed her gently and went for punch. Beau grinned like a sap. Could a man get any happier than his uncle? Any happier than he? Beau didn't think so, but he went in search of his wife and daughter, anyway.

Ever since they'd been reunited, body and soul, he couldn't spend enough time with both of them. He found them finally in the house, sitting quietly on the living room sofa. Callie's head rested in her mommy's lap. Her eyes were closed, her long ebony lashes gentle against her creamy peach cheeks. She'd ended up exhausted after the excitement of the day. Deedra stroked Callie's chin-length hair, a look of such contentment on her beautiful face his chest swelled with joy.

DEEDRA STROKED Callie's hair, loving the length, the natural blue-black hue, the soft, satiny feel. She thanked God for every minute of every day that this child had been returned to them. Thanked God that she'd finally found the path to trust. She'd finally been able to give her heart completely to her little girl and to her little girl's daddy.

She glanced up and saw him standing there, the love of her life, and her pulse danced. He still walked with a slight limp. Always would. It served to remind them to never take for granted the glorious gifts of their lives or their love.

Beau sat down beside Deedra and gathered a lock of his daughter's hair in his coarse fingers. "How's she doing?"

"Great." Every day Callie did better. She had never been shy before she'd been taken. But when she'd first come home, she'd been frightened, distrustful and clingy. Her age and a child's natural resilience were turning that around rapidly. "It's been quite a day for her."

"Quite a day for all three of us," the quaver in his voice said it all.

Today Callie had called Beau "Daddy" for the first time. Deedra had relived the memory again and again, and each time it brought tears to her eyes.

"How are you feeling, Mommy?" Beau's hand slipped over her rounding belly. She was three months pregnant. Same as Cassidy. The surgeon's good news the day of her hysterectomy had been that he'd only had to remove the noncancerous tumor, not her uterus. It had been textbook procedure, he'd said. She'd not only be able to conceive again, but likely have a normal pregnancy.

So far everything was going right.

"Cassidy had an ultrasound this week," Beau said. "She told Sean today that they're having a little girl. He's over the moon."

Deedra pulled his head to her, and she nuzzled his cheek. "Do you suppose we could go to bed now? I'd really like to show you how a wedding night ought to be celebrated."

"Why, Mrs. Shanahan, what a nice, naughty suggestion." Beau chuckled lustily. "But, since we're hosting this hoedown, I think we could disappear for an hour or so and not be missed, but longer than that would be bad manners, lady."

She gave him her most innocent round-eyed look. "My mama didn't teach me no good manners, sir."

His grin sent a zing of need through her.

He gathered Callie into his arms. "First tell me when you're getting *your* ultrasound. I want to be there."

She blew out a shuddery breath. "I had my ultrasound this week, too. I've been saving the news for after the wedding and reception. I didn't want anything to take away from Sean and Cassidy's special day."

Beau's gaze flashed from emerald to jade and filled with concern. "Is everything okay? Are *you* okay?"

"I'm perfect."

He sighed, his shoulders loosening. He caught her face gently in both hands and kissed her soundly. Then he gazed at her again, a different concern crossing his face. "The baby?"

She couldn't contain either her smile or the excitement for one more second. Her secret news burst out now. "Bab*ies*."

Beau jerked back, his ebony brows arching. "Babies? As in more than one?"

"It seems, Sheriff Shanahan, that we're having twins."

"Twins?" The idea seemed to stun him, but he quickly recovered. His smile grew as big as a Montana moon and his chest puffed with male pride. ''Yeah, twins. All right!''

Deedra laughed from her very heart, a warm musical chime of joy that brought a glow to her face and a grin to Beau's sexy mouth. ''That's right, cowboy. We're having two 'scrappin' Shanahan sons' to carry on the family name.''

HARLEQUIN®
INTRIGUE®

No cover charge.
No I.D. required.
Secrecy guaranteed.

**You're on
the guest list
for the hottest
romantic-suspense
series from**

PATRICIA ROSEMOOR

A team of outcast specialists with their own dark secrets has banded together at Chicago's hottest nightclub to defend the innocent...and find love and redemption along the way.

VELVET ROPES
July 2004

ON THE LIST
August 2004

Look for them wherever Harlequin books are sold!

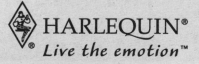

HARLEQUIN®
® Live the emotion™

www.eHarlequin.com

USA TODAY **bestselling author**

ERICA SPINDLER

Jane Killian has everything to live for. She's the toast of the Dallas art community, she and her husband, Ian, are completely in love—and overjoyed that Jane is pregnant.

Then her happiness shatters as her husband becomes the prime suspect in a murder investigation. Only Jane knows better. She knows that this is the work of the same man who stole her sense of security seventeen years ago, and now he's found her again… and he won't rest until he can *See Jane Die*…

SEE JANE DIE

"Creepy and compelling, *In Silence* is a real page-turner."
—*New Orleans Times-Picayune*

Available in June 2004 wherever books are sold.

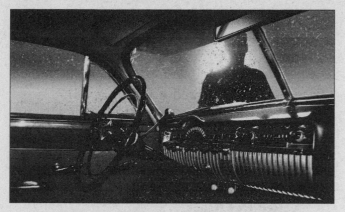

ED GORMAN
EVERYBODY'S SOMEBODY'S FOOL

A SAM McCAIN MYSTERY

When local bad boy David Egan is accused of murder, lawyer Sam McCain finds himself saddled with a new client…and another tale of small-town murder in Black River Falls, Iowa.

But McCain's client dies a fiery death in a car accident—an event that becomes murder when it's discovered the car's brake lines were cut. Working to clear Egan's name, McCain follows a trail of shattered dreams, cheating spouses, dark secrets to a body lying lifeless in a bath and to a tale of murder that embraces the vast human emotions that drive lovers to love…and killers to kill.

"…a fascinating time machine, recalling the arcana of a more innocent time.'
—Publishers Weekly

Available June 2004 at your favorite retail outlet.

 WORLDWIDE LIBRARY ®

WEG494

Harlequin Romance®

THE WEDDING PLANNERS

Where weddings are all in a day's work!

Have you ever wondered about the women behind the scenes, the ones who make those special days happen, the ones who help to create a memory built on love that lasts forever—who, no matter how expert they are at helping others, can't quite sort out their love lives for themselves?

Meet Tara, Skye and Riana—three sisters whose jobs consist of arranging the most perfect and romantic weddings imaginable—and read how they find themselves walking down the aisle with their very own Mr. Right…!

Don't miss the THE WEDDING PLANNERS trilogy by Australian author Darcy Maguire:

A Professional Engagement HR#3801

On sale June 2004 in Harlequin Romance®!

Plus:

The Best Man's Baby, HR#3805, on sale July 2004
A Convenient Groom, HR#3809, on sale August 2004

Available at your favorite retail outlet.

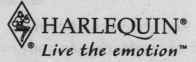

HARLEQUIN®
Live the emotion™

Visit us at www.eHarlequin.com

HRTWP

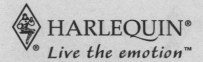